"You asked for it."

"And you damned well asked for this." Lucas took her mouth in bruising, hungry passion.

It was a kiss like no other Catriona had ever received. She wasn't exactly inexperienced when it came to kissing, and had known passion, eagerness and even something close to adoration. But never before had she been subjected to an indomitable will that steamrollered any resistance, and overpowered her senses.

SALLY WENTWORTH was born and raised in Hertfordshire, England, where she still lives, and started writing after attending an evening writing course. She is married and has one son. There is always a novel on the bedside table, but Sally also loves craft work, plays bridge and is the president of a National Trust group. Sometimes she doesn't know how she finds the time to write!

Books by Sally Wentworth

HARLEQUIN PRESENTS
1550—THE GOLDEN GREEK
1572—STORMY VOYAGE
1605—THE WAYWARD WIFE
1634—MIRRORS OF THE SEA
1668—YESTERDAY'S AFFAIR
1701—PRACTISE TO DECEIVE
1738—SHADOW PLAY

SALLY WENTWORTH

Duel in the Sun

Harlequin Books

TORONTO • NEW YORK • LONDON
AMSTERDAM • PARIS • SYDNEY • HAMBURG
STOCKHOLM • ATHENS • TOKYO • MILAN
MADRID • WARSAW • BUDAPEST • AUCKLAND

ISBN 0-373-11764-7

DUEL IN THE SUN

First North American Publication 1995.

CHAPTER ONE

IT WAS almost midnight when the plane landed at Luxor, bumping down on to the runway. The passengers, pleased that it had arrived ahead of schedule, eagerly collected up their hand luggage and waited to disembark. Catriona was seated towards the rear of the plane but considered herself lucky to be on it, only a last-minute cancellation making a seat available for her.

She left the plane in her turn, blinking to adjust her eyes to the warm, velvety darkness outside. It had been a charter flight, full of holidaymakers, who now hurried to go through Customs and get on the coaches waiting to take them on to their hotels or cruise boats. Catriona followed more slowly; the tourists were here for only a week or two, but she was staying for much longer and was laden with the bag containing her equipment, as well as a hold-all and a bag of duty-free drinks. An impassive customs officer stamped her passport, she found a trolley and collected her luggage from the carousel, then walked through to the front of the airport in the wake of the others.

There was some confusion at first because a couple of coaches hadn't yet arrived, but soon the couriers were shepherding away their flocks of tourists. Catriona stood to one side, looking for a smaller means of transport: a four-wheel-drive vehicle, or possibly a pick-up truck. One by one the buses filled and left, until she was standing alone under the harsh lights of the entrance. It was suddenly very quiet, the grinding noise of the coach engines fading in the distance. She stirred, beginning to feel

uneasy. Back in England that morning, as soon as she'd
known she was able to get a seat on the flight, Catriona
had telephoned the head of the Egyptology department
at the university, and he had promised to telephone the
excavation headquarters in Egypt so that someone could
meet her. But what if everyone at the dig was out? What
if the message hadn't got through? She certainly didn't
like the idea of just waiting here indefinitely.

Pushing her trolley back into the concourse, she saw
a man who looked European and went up to him.
'Excuse me? Do you speak English?' And when he
nodded, 'Are you from Dr Kane? From the dig at Mem
Habu?'

He shook his head. 'No, I'm sorry. I work here at the
airport.'

Catriona thanked him and went back outside. Still no
car. I'll give them half an hour, she decided, then I'll
have to try and find out the number and phone the dig
myself.

There was nowhere to sit. Catriona pulled her trolley
over to the wall and leaned against it, tired after her
journey and the mad rush to get ready for it. Over near
the car park there were two taxis optimistically waiting
for fares, their drivers leaning on one of them as they
chatted. The two men had glanced across at her several
times, and after a while one came over.

He was young, dark-skinned, and had a flashing smile.
'You wish taxi?' he enquired, his eyes running over her.

Catriona shook her head. Fat chance, when she hadn't
had time to get any Egyptian currency. And even if she
had, she would certainly have hesitated before she'd trust
herself to this man.

But he reached out to get hold of the trolley. 'I take
you Luxor.'

'No, thank you.' She made it sound very definite. 'I
am waiting for a car.'

'No car come now. I take you.'

Catriona grabbed the trolley. 'No! I have no money,' she told him, hoping he would be put off.

But he evidently didn't believe her because the man just shrugged and said again, 'I take you.'

For a couple of minutes they had a tug-of-war with the trolley, the man laughing at her, but then a car drove up, its engine so quiet as to be almost inaudible. Catriona didn't notice it until it stopped and the driver got out. He said something in Arabic, so sharply that the taxi driver immediately swung round, saw the car, and hurried back to his cab.

He had let go of the trolley so suddenly that Catriona fell back against the wall, but she quickly recovered and looked again at the car. She gave a sigh of disappointment; it was a big, black Mercedes, new and luxurious, certainly not the type of car that would be owned by a dig. But the driver came up to her and said in very broken English, 'You lady from England?'

Catriona nodded. 'Why, yes.'

'You come work here?' he added slowly, to make sure.

'Yes, I have.'

Satisfied, he said, 'I take you house.'

Thankful that her lift had arrived at last, Catriona went to help him load her luggage, but he held the back door of the car for her to get in, and loaded everything himself. The car was gorgeous, the upholstery of soft leather that still smelt new, the windows tinted, and it had the coolness that could only come from air-conditioning. Settling back into her seat, Catriona gave a sigh of relief; she had started to get a bit worried back there. Not that anything would have happened, of course; she need only have screamed to bring the airport guards hurrying out to help her. But it would hardly have been a good start to her stay in Egypt, especially if the field director got to hear of it. She had heard, back in England, that Dr Kane had no time for fools, and she had an idea that having to be guarded at the airport would definitely put her under that heading. Although it would have been his own fault, of course; he shouldn't have kept her waiting.

Thankfully pushing the imaginary scenario out of her mind, Catriona had to admit that Dr Kane had certainly made up for his tardiness by sending this car. She had expected a bumpy ride in an old truck, or a jeep at best.

The driver got in and soon they had left the airport buildings behind and were purring along in the darkness. 'Is it far?' she asked him.

He shrugged, not understanding.

Leaning forward, Catriona said clearly, 'The house; how long? How many miles, kilometres?'

Lifting his hand, he opened and closed it five times.

Twenty-five, then. But whether that was minutes, miles or kilometres she had no idea. And anyway, what did it matter? It was nice to just relax and stretch her long legs in luxurious comfort, so different from the cramped sardine tin of the plane. There was nothing to see outside; the night was completely dark except for the odd street lamp at a road-junction. Soon Catriona's eyelids drooped and she fell asleep.

'Lady. Lady!'

Opening her eyes, Catriona found that the driver had the door open and was trying to wake her. She sat up quickly, realising that they must have reached the ex-cavation house, where all the members of the team lived. Glancing at her watch as she got out of the car, Catriona saw that it was nearly two in the morning. Presumably everyone would be in bed by now. Expecting to be in some desert village, she glanced round in surprise at finding herself in front of a large house with what looked to be a garden all round it. The door of the house was standing open and a woman was waiting to greet her.

The woman was obviously Egyptian, but she wore a very severe Western-style dress with long sleeves, a high-neck, and the skirt low on her calves. She was middle-aged, too old to be the wife of one of the team, so perhaps she was some sort of housekeeper. She beckoned. 'You come, lady.'

She led the way into the house, but Catriona paused in the hallway to stand and stare. The house was sumptuous, there was no other word for it. The hall was high and richly decorated, with ornate Italian-looking furniture and a Venetian glass chandelier.

'Lady.'

The housekeeper again beckoned her on, leading her up a wide staircase to a galleried landing, the driver following them with the luggage. She turned to the right, went through a doorway into a corridor, and out on to another gallery, this time overlooking a big central courtyard in which a fountain played. It was dimly lit, so Catriona couldn't see very much, but even in the semi-darkness it looked a delightful place. Opening a door a few rooms down, the woman indicated that she should go in.

Catriona caught her breath; the room was the complete opposite to what she had expected. Again it was luxuriously furnished, although much too opulently for her English taste, with a large gold-painted bed, big wardrobes, and a dressing-table wide enough to accommodate a chorus line. Everything seemed to be on a large scale, as if big was beautiful. But it looked so comfortable and was so cool that Catriona was more than grateful. And there was even her own bathroom, as the woman demonstrated when she opened a door in the right-hand wall. The bath was so huge that Catriona couldn't help but laugh.

The woman frowned, not understanding, but Catriona gave her a big smile and she relaxed again.

'Breakfast?' Catriona said to her, and mimed eating. 'What time?' and she pointed to her watch.

Spreading her hands, the woman shrugged, then showed her a bell-push within reach of the bed. Using signs, she got through to Catriona that she must push the bell and the woman would bring her breakfast. She left her then, and Catriona sat on the edge of the high bed and kicked off her shoes. The house and the car were certainly a revelation; she had always been under the impression that excavation teams were housed in almost primitive conditions, were so under-funded that they had to watch every penny. But whoever was sponsoring this team must have been terrifically generous.

Going into the bathroom, Catriona showered and wrapped herself in one of the huge, soft bath-sheets, then again laughed aloud at the sheer luxury of it all. Back home, she had been so hard up and desperate for work that she had jumped at the chance of this job, been prepared to take it on however rough the conditions. But if she'd only known that she was going to live in a place like this she wouldn't have hesitated even for a moment; she was only surprised that someone with more experience hadn't beaten her to it.

She slept deeply that night, the big bed soft and comfortable, the air-conditioning keeping the room at an even temperature. Waking around nine and remembering the instructions she'd been given, Catriona pressed the bell, and within a very short time the house-keeper carried in a large breakfast tray. There were two types of cereal, an omelette and tomatoes under a heated cover, rolls and strange-looking bread, fruit, and coffee. A feast! If they lived like this all the time, no wonder digs went on for years.

Feeling more optimistic than she had for ages, Catriona ate, and then dressed. Expecting to go out into the desert to the dig, she put on a pair of cream cotton trousers, with a complementary short-sleeved blouse. Then she sat down at the dressing-table to brush her long, corn-gold hair and weave it into a plait, and thought about the rumours she'd heard of Dr Lucas Kane and decided they must have arisen out of jealousy. His reputation as a slave-driver must certainly be wrong; having breakfast in bed brought to her and allowing her to sleep in to recover from her journey definitely weren't the acts of a petty tyrant.

She looked at herself critically in the mirror, wondering whether or not to put on make-up. Her skin was pale from a long English winter and from working long hours for a clothing company until she'd been fired, the owner still owing her a month's pay. Luckily her eyelashes were long and dark, in arresting contrast to her hair, and making an attractive frame to her hazel eyes. Her face, though, was thinner than it should have been, the result of overwork and not enough nourishing food since she'd lost the job, nearly three months ago. But the thinness emphasised the good bone-structure of her heart-shaped face, the eyes wide and candid, her cheekbones high, which, with her delicate mouth, gave Catriona a look of almost fragile elegance.

It was a deceptive look; life had been tough and she'd had to fight for everything she had achieved, both at school and at college. Not that her qualifications had been of much good getting her the job she wanted, she thought ruefully, but then brightened; until now. If she could make a success of this job that had landed so unexpectedly in her lap, who knew where it might lead? If nothing else, she would have a useful addition to her CV.

Coming to a decision, Catriona added lipstick and powder, and left it at that. As she was blotting her lip-

stick there was a knock at the door. Expecting it to be
the housekeeper, she called, 'Come in.'

The door was opened slowly, and to Catriona's surprise, a child, a little girl, looked tentatively in. She
looked at Catriona, caught her involuntary smile, and
moved back out of sight. There was the sound of whispering, then two heads came round the door, the second
that of another little girl and at a lower height than the
first. Two pairs of eyes, large and dark, regarded her
shyly.

Catriona turned to face them, again smiling. 'Hello.'
She held out a hand and beckoned them in.

Slowly they came into the room, clutching hands, the
younger with her finger in her mouth. The elder child
looked about nine, the other about four years younger.
It was evident that they were sisters; their features were
very much alike, and they both had dark, plaited hair,
and wore identical dark blue dresses with white collars
and cuffs, and long white socks. Severe clothes for such
young children, Catriona thought, but maybe it was their
school uniform.

'Hello,' she said again.

'Hello, lady.' It was the elder one who spoke, her face
grave, voice uncertain.

'What is your name?' Catriona asked, pointing and
speaking slowly and clearly.

'I Nadia.'

'And what is your name?' Looking at the younger
child.

But the little girl only blushed shyly and hid behind
her sister.

'She Dorreya,' the elder girl supplied.

'My name is Catriona,' repeating slowly at their
uncomprehending looks, 'Cat-ri-on-a.'

First the elder and then the younger child repeated it
several times until they had it right. Then there were

smiles of pleasure all round. They must be the children of one of the Egyptian members of the team, Catriona surmised. Another knock sounded at the door and the housekeeper looked in. When she saw the children she began to scold and to shoo them away.

'Oh, no,' Catriona protested. 'Let them stay, they aren't in the way.'

But the woman took no notice, shutting the door behind the children. She turned to Catriona who had risen from her seat, looked her up and down, and burst into a stream of Arabic, gesturing at her clothes. Not understanding a word, Catriona only shrugged. Talking again, the housekeeper touched her trousers and blouse, shaking her head. 'No, no.' Then she went to the wardrobe, opened it, found a skirt and long-sleeved shirt and brought them out, making signs that Catriona should put them on.

'Why?' Catriona asked in astonishment.

Another flood of Arabic that she didn't understand, but it was obvious what the woman wanted, and even more obvious that it was important to her, so, with a shrug, Catriona changed into the skirt, but she drew the line at the blouse; it would be far too hot when she got outside. The housekeeper had decorously turned her back, but pushed the shirt towards her when she looked round.

Catriona shook her head. 'No. Too hot.'

Again the woman tried to persuade her, the word *pasha* coming into it quite a lot, but when Catriona continued to stubbornly shake her head the woman looked at her watch, lifted her hands into the air in a gesture of angry surrender, and said, 'You come.'

So she was to meet the team, or at least some of them; presumably most of them were out at the dig. Perhaps Dr Kane had come to meet and brief her on her duties. Catriona hoped, anxiously, that he would find her satisfactory; it was a while since she had left college and she hadn't had a chance to do any practical work in ancient textile conservation in the last two years. But she had studied the subject and had been madly reading it up again during the last week, ever since she knew she might be coming here.

Catriona wasn't looking forward to meeting Dr Kane. She wasn't exactly nervous; wary would probably be a better word. It wasn't just because of his reputation as a hard taskmaster—Catriona enjoyed working hard— but she'd also heard that he set very high standards, and to get this job she'd had to exaggerate her practical experience rather. Still, now that she was here they would have to give her a chance to prove herself, she thought optimistically. But she didn't much like the idea of working for someone who insisted on his female staff wearing skirts. Dr Kane must be really dated and old!

The housekeeper led the way down to the central courtyard where the fountain played. It was open to the sky, a shaded garden of flowering tropical plants and the musical tinkling of splashing water. They crossed the courtyard and the woman knocked at a door, then opened it for Catriona to go in. It was a library, lined with shelves of richly bound books. Catriona walked into the room expecting to meet an elderly Englishman. But the man who looked up from his desk was quite young, dark-haired, and Egyptian.

The man's eyes went over her and widened. He put his pen down on the desk, his eyes taking her in, and it was a few moments before he said a formal, 'Good morning.'

'Good morning.' Catriona recovered quickly from her surprise. So Dr Kane hadn't bothered to meet her himself; this man must be their Egyptian liaison officer or something like that. Not that he looked much like an employee; he was wearing a well-cut and expensive-looking dark suit and a lot of jewellery: there was a thick gold watch on his wrist, and he wore several rings, one of them on his left hand with a stone that looked like a diamond but was too big to possibly be real. He looked to be in his late thirties, had olive skin and rounded features with the small beard favoured by Arabic men.

The Egyptian, who hadn't stood to greet her, was looking Catriona over with just as much interest, then said, 'You are much younger than I expected. I can hardly think that the details you sent about yourself can be correct.'

Aware of her magnified qualifications, Catriona said quickly, 'Oh, but I've had quite a lot of experience. I'm sure you'll find my work satisfactory.'

'How old are you?' he shot at her.

'I'm twenty-three. Nearly twenty-four,' she added hopefully.

The man picked up a piece of paper from his desk, glanced at it, then at her, his eyes cold. 'Then you can hardly have had the experience you claim in this record of your work. How can you possibly have spent——?'

He broke off as there was a knock at the door and the two little girls came in. Immediately his eyes softened, but he spoke to them rather reprovingly in Arabic, and Catriona guessed they were being told off for interrupting.

But Dorreya took no notice and ran to take hold of her hand. 'Cat-ri-on-a,' she said, dimpling up at her.

Catriona smiled and stooped down to the little girl's level. 'Hello, Dorreya.'

'Hell-o,' Dorreya repeated, and turned to the man with a big grin, to show how clever she was.

The Egyptian was watching, and at the same time stooping to listen as Nadia whispered in his ear. He looked thoughtful, then straightened. 'It seems you have met my daughters already.'

'Are they your children?' Catriona straightened and smiled at him. 'They're adorable. You must be very proud of them.'

'Yes, of course.' He was eyeing her again, and after a moment, turned to the children and gently shooed them away. When they'd gone, he said, 'It seems that they like you.'

'Thank you.'

'Perhaps,' he said, 'I will give you a trial. Although I cannot approve of anyone who has so blatantly lied about their qualifications.'

Catriona flushed a little; she hadn't thought it was that bad! Stiffly, she said, 'OK. When do I meet the rest of the team?'

'The team?' His eyebrows rose. 'There is no one else; you will be in sole charge.'

Catriona stared at him. 'But there must be other people?'

'No. The children are on holiday from school and are entirely your responsibility, although my housekeeper, Mrs Aziz, will always be here if you need her. Surely you understood that when you agreed to take the job, Miss Welland?'

An icy feeling crept into Catriona's chest and she swallowed. 'What—what did you call me?'

'Miss Welland,' he replied testily. 'It's your name, isn't it?'

Catriona slowly shook her head and looked at him unhappily. 'No. It isn't. I think—I rather think that there has been a mistake.'

It was the Egyptian's turn to stare. Then he said, 'Are you or are you not Miss Welland, of London, who applied for the position of English teacher to my children during the summer?'

'No, I'm not.'

His voice sharpened. 'Then just who are you—and what are you doing here?'

'I'm Catriona Fenton. I was waiting at the airport for someone to pick me up and your driver came and asked if I was from England and had come to work in Luxor. So naturally I said yes, and—well, here I am.'

'And did it not occur to you to ask the driver who had sent him?' the Egyptian demanded angrily.

'Didn't it occur to you to tell the driver to ask for this Miss Welland by name?' Catriona countered. 'He didn't ask who I was and he didn't speak much English.' The man stiffened, obviously unused to a woman standing up for herself, but Catriona didn't notice. Remembering her wait at the airport, she added, 'And anyway, it was a natural mistake on both sides because I was the only woman waiting from that flight.'

His eyes narrowed. 'There was no one else? No other English woman?'

Catriona shook her head. 'Definitely not.'

He muttered a sharp imprecation. 'What has happened to the woman? I have heard nothing from her.'

Catriona didn't know and didn't much care. Her thoughts were filled with dismay; presumably the transport from the dig had arrived at the airport after she'd left. Dr Kane must have thought that she, too, hadn't turned up and be cursing her as this Egyptian was now cursing his lost governess. If she wanted to stop Dr Kane sending out for someone else from England she had better get in touch with him at once, although how she was going to explain away being lost for almost a day, Catriona hated to think.

But the Egyptian gave a dismissive gesture and said, 'It is no matter. *You* will teach my children instead.'

Catriona laughed, unable to believe what she'd heard. 'That's ridiculous! I'm not a teacher.'

He frowned when she laughed, but said, 'You are
English and you speak well. It is all I want. And you
will be well paid. I agreed to give Miss Welland fifteen
thousand pounds for two months here, plus her air fare,
of course.'

Her mouth falling open, Catriona exclaimed, 'Fifteen
thousand pounds!' But then she realised. 'Oh, you mean
Egyptian pounds.' She did some rapid mental arith-
metic; it was still a lot of money, far more than she'd
been promised at the dig. But she shook her head. 'I'm
sorry, Mr... What *is* your name?'

The Egyptian seemed to square his shoulders and there
was inherent arrogance in his voice as he said, 'My name
is Omar Rafiq. And this house is the Garden of the
Nile—my country house.'

'Yes, well, Mr Rafiq, I'm sorry, I can't work for you
because I'm already committed to work at an excavation
site.'

'You are not a travel courier?'

'No. I'm a textile expert. I came out here at short
notice to take the place of someone who had to fly home
for family reasons. I couldn't possibly let them down.'
Even as she said it Catriona wondered if Dr Kane was
at this moment on the telephone to England, furiously
demanding to know where she was.

'You would not find the house where you live at the
excavation site pleasant,' Rafiq told her. Adding
imperiously, 'It is much better here, so you will stay.'

Even if Catriona had wanted the job, she would have
objected to the way he issued such peremptory orders.
Her mouth had dropped open at his insolence, but now
it hardened. 'I've already said no. I'm sorry about the
mix-up, but it was your driver who made the mistake,
and I must ask you to take me to the excavation site
straight away.'

He frowned angrily, but then shrugged and reached for a telephone on his desk. 'Where is it?'

'A place called Mem Habu. I believe it's to the north-west of Luxor and...' Her voice trailed off as she saw Omar Rafiq's head come up in surprise and his eyes widen.

'Are you talking of the excavation under the leadership of Lucas Kane?'

She nodded. 'Dr Kane. That's right. Do you know him?'

'We have—met.' He took his hand from the phone and leaned back in his chair. 'So you are Kane's new textile expert.' And he suddenly began to laugh.

Catriona didn't like the sound of that laughter. It had no humour in it, was more a triumphant peal. 'What's so funny?' she demanded.

Rafiq stopped laughing but there was still a mocking twist to his lips as he said, 'Just that you should be on your way there, of all places.'

She frowned. 'I don't understand.'

'It is no matter.' Rafiq gave her a contemplative look, his eyes again running over her tall, slim figure, settling on her face. Catriona had seen that assessing look in men's eyes a thousand times before, and it certainly wasn't the way Rafiq had looked at her when he'd thought her to be his children's tutor.

Her chin lifting, she said. 'I'll go and pack. Please tell your driver to take me to the site in half an hour.'

Again Rafiq looked amused. 'You would not be happy there, Miss Fenton. The site house is very primitive. And Dr Kane...' He spread his hands in a descriptive gesture and there was scarcely concealed dislike in his voice as he said, 'He is a quick-tempered man. You would not find him sympathetic, especially after going to the wrong place. I assure you, you would be much happier here.'

'No, thank you,' Catriona replied firmly. 'Will you tell your driver to take me or not?'

'I'm afraid he is busy today.'

It was a lie and they both knew it. Catriona glared at him, but Rafiq merely gave her a mocking, arrogant look in return. Anger filled her, but Catriona merely said, 'In that case I will take a taxi.'

He gave a sardonic smile. 'By all means.'

'Please call one for me.'

'If you wish to take a taxi, Miss Fenton, you must telephone yourself. Here is the directory.'

He took a thick book from a drawer in his desk and passed it to her. Catriona took it, her eyes on his face, not liking his expression one bit. Glancing down at the phone book, she began to flip through the pages but soon came to an angry stop. The whole book was, of course, in Arabic script, the loops and whirls completely incomprehensible to her western eyes. 'You know I can't read this,' she said shortly. 'Just what are you trying to do?'

'To keep you here, of course.' Standing up, Rafiq came round the desk. His smile losing its mockery, he turned on the charm and said persuasively, 'My children like you, Miss Fenton. And it would be a great inconvenience to send to England for another teacher for them. This house is, I think you'll agree, very comfortable, and the pay is good. In fact I will increase the amount, if you will stay, to——' again he looked at her contemplatively '—to twenty thousand pounds.'

Catriona had been short of money for so long that the offer was very tempting, but she had recognised that assessing glance and was pretty sure that the extra money was also a sweetener that might help to persuade her to become something more than just his children's tutor. But she definitely wasn't into that. She had the instinctive feeling that he was the kind of man who used

women, who had no real respect for her sex and looked
on them as there merely for his amusement or service.
And besides, his overbearing arrogance, his calm as-
sumption that she should just drop all her plans and do
what he wanted, had aroused a stubborn anger in her
that no amount of smooth charm could overcome, so
she said firmly, 'I've already said no. Please don't ask
me again. I've promised to work at the dig and I intend
to keep that promise. So please phone for a taxi.'

But Rafiq merely gave a small smile. 'Why don't you
think about it? Look round the house. There is a
swimming-pool outside. The children will show you. And
we will talk again over dinner.'

Becoming angry, Catriona said, 'Mr Rafiq, will you
please listen to me? I have to get to Mem Habu as soon
as possible. Dr Kane will be worried about me. He will
have phoned to England to see where I am.'

To her surprise he looked amused again, and she could
only guess that there was some sort of enmity between
the two men. 'I am sure Dr Kane can wait.'

She went to argue again but he had pressed a bell on
his desk and the children came back into the room. He
spoke to them in Arabic and they laughed and caught
Catriona's hands, eagerly pulling her out with them. For
a moment she tried to resist, turning to look at their
father, but Rafiq came up behind them and closed the
door, shutting her out with the children so the door
received the fuming look that had been meant for him.

Allowing the children to lead her round the house,
Catriona was shown the swimming-pool, the indoor
tennis court and gymnasium, was taken round the
courtyard garden, and finally up to a big sitting-room
on the first floor which had a wide veranda. From it
there was the most marvellous view of the River Nile,
only a couple of hundred yards away. It was her first
glimpse of the famous river, and Catriona stood in fas-

cination, watching a small fleet of feluccas, their sails bleached by the sun, sail slowly by.

Mrs Aziz came into the room and spoke to the children. Nadia turned to Catriona. 'We go...' She mimed washing her face and hands.

'To wash,' Catriona supplied.

The little girls repeated it after her and ran out of the room. Mrs Aziz went to follow but Catriona caught her arm. 'Please. You speak English?'

The woman shrugged. 'Little.'

There was a phone on a table by the wall. Gesturing to it, Catriona said, 'You telephone for me. Ask for a taxi.'

But the housekeeper shook her head vigorously. 'No. Pasha Omar, he say no taxi.'

'Please,' Catriona pleaded. 'I shouldn't be here. I must go.'

But the woman was obviously intimidated by her employer; she refused to be persuaded and pulled away, then hurried from the room.

Catriona bit her lip in vexation; this was starting to get out of hand. And she couldn't understand why. She was sure that Rafiq had accepted her refusal and had been about to let her go, but then she'd mentioned Dr Kane and everything had changed. For a few minutes she felt helpless, a stranger lost in a strange land, but then her natural confidence returned to her; this was almost the twenty-first century, and there was no way anyone could keep her here against her will. Crossing to the phone, she picked up the receiver, then realised she didn't know what number to dial to get the operator, but she tried various combinations and at last got a ringing tone. A voice came on the line and Catriona said quickly, 'Please, do you speak English?'

The operator didn't, but eventually found someone who did. 'Can I help you?'

'Can you give me the number of a taxi company? I need a taxi.'

'Where are you?'

'Near Luxor.'

'Dial this number.' The operator read out a list of digits which Catriona hastily wrote down.

Again she had to wait while someone who spoke English was found, then she asked for a taxi to take her to Mem Habu. 'Where do you wish to be picked up?'

'At the house of Omar Rafiq. It's called the Garden of the Nile.'

'What district?'

'I don't know the district. Can't you look the address up in the phone book?'

'How can we come if we do not know the address?'

'Please try,' Catriona begged. 'It is most important. An emergency. I must have a taxi.'

'We will try,' the voice conceded, then the line went dead.

Catriona put the phone down with a sigh of relief. At last she was getting somewhere. She had no idea how long it would take the taxi to get here, but she went immediately to her room and repacked all her things, but was afraid to take them downstairs in case Rafiq saw them and guessed what she was doing.

At one, Nadia came to take her to lunch and she thought it best to go, to allay any suspicions Rafiq might have. But he wasn't there; only Mrs Aziz and the children were waiting in a small dining-room. Throughout the meal, while she was trying to talk to the children, Catriona listened for the sound of the doorbell, ready to rush out and grab the taxi, make him wait while she collected her things. But the bell didn't ring. She tried to find out the exact address of the house, but Mrs Aziz had evidently been ordered not to tell her, and stopped Nadia from doing so.

The meal ended and the children went to their rooms for a siesta. Catriona went down to the entrance hall and sat down in one of the Italian chairs to wait for the taxi, no longer caring whether Rafiq saw her or not.

She waited all afternoon but still it didn't come.

Around four-thirty Omar Rafiq came into the hall and stood in front of her. He looked amused. 'There is no point in waiting any longer, Miss Fenton. I rang the taxi company immediately after you had made the call and told them that you had made a mistake.'

'You mean you listened to my call?'

He smiled unpleasantly. 'Of course. I told them that you were ill—with sunstroke, and that they were to ignore you if you made any more calls.'

Catriona had expected as much for the last two hours. She got to her feet, her eyes bitter. 'Are you aware of the penalty for kidnapping—because that's what this is?'

Rafiq laughed contemptuously. 'Nonsense, Miss Fenton. I am only trying to persuade you to accept the post I am offering you.'

'Not persuade—coerce,' she corrected him.

He gave a small smile. 'You have proved my point; your command of English is excellent.'

'So is yours. Why don't you teach your children yourself?'

'Unfortunately I do not have the time. My business is in Cairo. I come here for only a few days at a time.'

Deciding to have one more go at persuasion, Catriona said, 'Look, Mr Rafiq, I'm sorry your English tutor didn't turn up, but maybe I'll be able to help you; I have several friends in England who might be interested in this job. If you like I could phone them and——'

'But I want you to teach them, so there is no point,' he interrupted impatiently. Then, using moral blackmail, he said, 'Don't you like my daughters?'

'Yes, of course, but——'

'Don't you like this house? Is your room not comfortable?'

'Yes, but——'

'Aren't the wages I am offering you more than those you would earn at the excavation?'

Fearing another interruption, Catriona said firmly, 'Money isn't of the first concern. The job at the site would be a great help in my career; teaching your children wouldn't.'

'Your career? Of what importance will that be when you marry?'

'I'm not about to get married.'

'You will in time. All girls get married,' he said sweepingly. Catriona gave a gasp of astonishment; the man was still in the Dark Ages! 'So, Miss Fenton,' he repeated, 'I insist that you stay.'

'No!'

'But you have no choice, do you?'

'This is—this is white slavery!' Catriona exclaimed furiously.

That made him laugh, which made her feel slightly ridiculous, but then even more angry at her own helplessness. Suddenly Rafiq seemed to become bored by the whole thing. 'Why do you not play with the children?' he said impatiently, but it was in the tone of an order, not a suggestion.

Having nothing else to do, Catriona went to find the girls. OK, she thought, I'll wait till it's dark and everyone's asleep, then I'll sneak out and walk to the nearest town and get a taxi from there. She took the children to the pool and, in order to safeguard them while they played in the water, had to put on a swimsuit and go in herself. It was OK until Rafiq arrived, but she didn't much like the idea of having on only a swimsuit with

him around. When he took off his robe, obviously
intending to join them in the water, Catriona quickly got
out and wrapped a large towel round her waist, sarong-
style.

Rafiq dived in and swam a few lengths in a strong
crawl, then came to play with the girls. That he adored
his daughters was plain enough; he was great with them,
pretending to chase them until they shrieked, but very
gentle when he caught them. Catriona couldn't help but
smile, but she caught him looking at her and remembered
that the games he played with little girls could be quite
different to those he played with big girls. She wondered
what had happened to the children's mother, but maybe
she was still in Cairo, awaiting her husband's return.

Mrs Aziz came to take the children away and Catriona
went to go with them, but Rafiq, standing at the pool's
edge, water trickling down his body, caught her arm and
said, 'You will dine with me tonight.' And it wasn't an
invitation.

She looked at him, wary, and becoming very apprehensive. No way was she going to spend another night
in this house. Catriona decided to try to sneak out before
dinner. But it would be better not to let him suspect, so
she merely said, 'OK. Where's the dining-room?'

'I will show you.' He put on a robe, led her into the
main entrance hall, and pointed to a door opening off
it. 'At eight-thirty,' he told her.

Catriona nodded and walked up the stairs to go to her
room. Rafiq stood in the hall watching her go, his thick
white robe hanging open.

Suddenly there was a commotion outside and then the
front door was pushed open, so violently that it went
crashing back on its hinges. A man strode into the hall.
A fair-haired European. Tall, broad-shouldered and with

arrogant self-assurance. Seeing Rafiq, he came to a stop and put his fists on his hips. A sardonic smile came to the man's lips and he said, 'Hello, Omar. I hear you've kidnapped my new textile expert!'

CHAPTER TWO

CATRIONA stood on the stairs, frozen with astonishment. Then a great feeling of relief filled her and she went to run down to the hall, but then stopped; Rafiq hadn't been so taken aback and had moved forward to face the intruder.

'Good evening, Dr Kane,' Rafiq said smoothly, apparently in no way put out. 'What a pleasant surprise.'

So this was Lucas Kane. Catriona stood still, hidden from Kane's sight by a bend in the stairs, but able to watch the two men as they confronted each other. Rafiq had an inborn hauteur that had probably grown through a hundred generations, but Kane had the self-confidence of a man who had carved out his own success in life. Physically Kane was much the taller of the two, a couple of inches over six feet, Catriona guessed, and where Rafiq was dark-haired and -skinned, he was fair, although he had a deep-golden tan that could only have come from long hours spent in the sun. Both men could have been called good-looking, but in entirely different ways; Rafiq's features were soft and would one day be full, but Kane's face would never be anything but lean, almost hawk-like. The Egyptian's eyes were dark and long-lashed, those of Kane an intense slate grey.

'A surprise, Omar?' Kane answered, his eyebrows rising. 'But surely you knew I wouldn't let you get away with it?'

To Catriona's surprise, Rafiq laughed. 'It was purely a mistake, my dear Dr Kane. And entirely your own fault. You really should make sure that you're on time, you know. The lady waited so long for you that when my car arrived to collect someone else she thought it was for her and was brought here. Naturally she was made most welcome.'

'And why didn't you phone to tell me of the—er—mistake?'

'I didn't find it out myself until I met the lady—this morning.' His deliberate pause emphasised that it was now evening.

'And since then?' Kane queried.

Rafiq gave a small smile, knowing that Catriona was listening. 'Why, the lady has been having a very pleasant time, enjoying my house, my hospitality. In fact I've been trying to persuade her to stay here——' again he paused as Dr Kane's head came sharply up '—as an English teacher for my children, of course.'

'And has the lady yielded to your persuasion?' Kane asked sardonically.

'Oh, come now, Dr Kane, you do not really expect me to tell you that, do you?' Catriona made an angry movement and Rafiq turned quickly in her direction. 'But why don't you ask her for yourself? Please, Catriona, come down.' And he added, 'There is no need to be afraid of Dr Kane; he will not harm you—*in my house*.' This last on a definitely mocking note.

Slowly Catriona came further down the stairs until Kane could see her. Her hair had got wet while she was swimming and she had undone the plait, shaking her hair loose so it could dry. The dampness had made it curl so that it framed her face and hung in twisting, golden tendrils that caressed her bare shoulders. Kane's eyes widened and he stared at her face in arrested surprise, but then he glanced down and saw how little she was wearing and his expression changed. His eyes swept over her and then, noticing Rafiq's partly open robe, hardened and became contemptuous. Catriona pulled the towel tighter around her, feeling strangely indecent under his scornful gaze.

'Well?' Kane said harshly. 'Has he persuaded you to stay?'

Her chin came up. 'No. Of course not.'

Kane's left eyebrow rose in surprise at her forcefulness and his gaze lingered for a moment on her face, on the tilt of her chin. Turning to Rafiq, he said jeeringly, 'It seems as if you're losing your touch, Omar.'

Rafiq shrugged eloquently. 'Catriona has been here only one day; perhaps when she has seen your house she will change her mind.'

'Not if she has any sense.'

'But she is so fragile, so delicate.' Rafiq used his hands eloquently and this time both men's eyes turned to look her over. 'I'm afraid she will find life in your primitive house far too hard, and then she will——'

Tired of being talked about as if she wasn't there, Catriona cut in, 'I've already said that I don't want to stay here. I want to go to the dig.'

'So instead of just standing there, why don't you go and put some clothes on?' Kane demanded scathingly.

Catriona shot him an angry look, beginning to realise why he had such a tyrannical reputation. 'My cases are already packed; I'll be down in just a few minutes,' she said shortly, and turned to run back up the stairs to her room. Hastily she towelled herself dry and dressed, found a bag for her wet swimsuit and shoved it in her case. She couldn't manage all her luggage alone; going through on to the galleried landing, she looked over. The two men were standing close together and seemed to be in the middle of a heated but low-voiced argument. Catriona called, 'Would one of you help me with my cases, please?' and they moved apart.

Rafiq gestured to one of his servants who was waiting near the open door and the man came to help her. When she followed him down she found that Dr Kane had gone outside to wait. Rafiq, too, was waiting. Taking her hand, he didn't shake it, but bowed over it. 'You have graced my house, Catriona. And I am sure that you will again.'

'I doubt it,' she returned shortly.

He smiled. 'Wait until you have seen the house at the excavation site. My offer is still open and you will soon be back, Catriona.'

Realising that he couldn't be argued with, she merely said, 'I didn't say you could call me that.'

'But I am going to. And I want you to call me Omar.'

'As I won't be seeing you again, there won't be any need, will there? Goodbye.'

She turned to leave and saw that Dr Kane had stepped back into the doorway and had heard. He laughed, but waited until Catriona had got into the passenger seat of the waiting Land Rover and he had climbed in beside her before he leaned out of the window and called jeeringly, 'It seems the lady wasn't tempted, Omar. You'll just have to make your bribes bigger in future!' Laughing again, he gunned the car down the driveway and through the heavy wooden gates of the Garden of the Nile.

The Land Rover bumped along the worn-surfaced road, making Catriona grab for the dashboard to brace herself. The car was old and noisy, and the seat had long ago lost its stuffing. It was so exactly what she had originally expected that she laughed aloud.

Dr Kane glanced across at her. 'What's so funny?'

She shook her head. 'It's nothing.'

He thumped an angry fist on the steering-wheel. 'Why the hell do women always say that when you ask them a question?' he demanded. 'Is it because you think I won't understand the subtleties of the female mind—or is it just that your mind is a complete blank? "It's nothing",' he mimicked, falsetto. 'When I ask you a question, woman, you damn well answer it! Is that understood?'

His manner would have intimidated most women, but not Catriona. She was still overpoweringly grateful that he had rescued her from Omar. And had done it in such a satisfyingly high-handed way, too; leaving Omar discomfited on his own doorstep. She was still on a high from that, full of a crazy kind of excitement that shone in her eyes. But she managed to say calmly enough, 'I was laughing at the age and discomfort of this car; it was exactly what I originally expected to be met by.'

'So why on earth were you stupid enough to go off in Omar's limo?' Dr Kane asked scornfully.

'Why didn't you send someone to collect me?' she countered, determined not to grovel.

'I did. You'd gone.'

'I waited for ages,' she said accusingly.

Her words were almost drowned under the noise of the hooter as a truck, loaded with live camels, of all things, got in the way. She thought he hadn't heard, but when they'd passed the truck, he said, as if it was her fault, 'You were early. The planes are late so regularly that no one bothers to get there until half an hour after one's due in.'

'I suppose nobody bothered to phone and check?'

A warning glint came into Kane's eyes. 'Don't push it; I had a devil of a job tracking you down.'

'How *did* you find me?'

'By making enquiries at the airport. But I had to wait till the night shift came back on before I heard you'd gone in Omar's car. Of all the damn stupid things to do!'

Stiffly, Catriona said, 'I'm sorry if I caused any in-convenience, Dr Kane, but it was——'

'Lucas,' he interrupted. 'My name's Lucas Kane. There's no formality at the dig. And, yes, you were a damn nuisance. An official at the airport confirmed that you'd arrived but I had to bribe a taxi-driver before I found out where you'd gone.'

'Bribe him?' Catriona was shocked. 'I hope you didn't have to pay him too much?'

'Enough—and I'm taking it out of your wages.'

She should have expected that. Catriona grinned inwardly, and sat back in her seat. The Land Rover had slowed, caught up in a snarl of traffic on the outskirts of a town. Luxor, she supposed. It was almost dark but the streets were still full of cars, taxis, tourist buses, as well as bicycles, rickety old trucks, horse-drawn buggies, and people who just stepped out into the street to cross whenever they felt like it. Everyone seemed to drive on their horns; it was hot, dusty, noisy and intensely foreign. Magic!

Dr Kane—no, Lucas, had to concentrate and she was able to sit quietly and look him over. Closer to, he wasn't so fair as she'd first thought; his hair was brown but had been bleached by the sun, as if he didn't bother to wear a hat. He had a natural air of authority and she guessed that he didn't often need to browbeat his staff. Catriona wondered why he had with her; to show her how angry he was, perhaps, or maybe just because she was female and needed to be put in her place. Fleetingly she wondered if he was married, then decided he couldn't be. He didn't act as if he'd been gentled by constant female company. He hadn't offered to carry her luggage or open the car door for her, hadn't asked if she'd had a good flight. And even more important, hadn't asked if Omar Rafiq had attempted to coerce her to stay. But maybe he didn't have to ask; maybe he knew.

There was hostility between the two men; she'd not only sensed it but had seen it in their eyes, their actions. On the surface it was like verbal fencing, but she wondered what it would take and what passions would be

unleashed if they ever came to open enmity. And she
was intrigued to know what had caused two such dis-
similar men to have clashed in the first place.

They had circled the outskirts of the town and the
traffic wasn't so heavy now. Some of the cars they passed
had lights on, some hadn't bothered; it seemed to be a
matter of personal taste—or perhaps just whether the
lights worked. Her eyes flicked back to Lucas's hard
profile.

'So what are your conclusions?' he asked in a conversational tone.

'On what subject?' she asked warily.

'Me. You've been studying me long enough.'

She blinked, taken aback, but thought she might as
well satisfy her curiosity, so said, 'I was wondering why
you and Omar Rafiq were so—abrasive.'

'Abrasive!' He laughed. 'A good word. I have no
reason to like him.'

'Why not?'

He gave her an assessing look. 'Why the interest?'

Catriona shrugged. 'I'd like to know what you rescued
me from.'

'Wouldn't he let you leave?'

'No.'

Lucas laughed again, really amused this time. 'I
suppose you had visions of ending up in his harem. Did
you tell him you were headed for my dig?'

'Yes, of course.'

'That's why, then; he only wanted to keep you there
to inconvenience me.'

An egotistical remark that Catriona found extremely
annoying. 'What if I'd decided to stay?'

With a shrug, Lucas said, 'It's hypothetical; you
didn't.'

'He offered me far more money than you're paying
me. Double, in fact,' she goaded.

'Then you were a fool not to accept,' he returned calmly.

Catriona let him negotiate a busy road junction, then said, 'You still haven't told me why you don't like him.'

'I know I haven't.'

'So why?'

He shot her a frowning glance. 'What an extremely nosy woman you are. Do you really want to know about excavation politics so soon?'

'Yes.'

His lips twitched a little at her unequivocal response. 'All right, if you must know; Omar offered to sponsor the dig but then backed out at the last minute.'

So that was all it was about, just money. Catriona felt a fleeting moment of disappointment, which changed to anger when she realised she had been used as a pawn in their disagreement. Had Omar, then, merely been amusing himself by trying to frighten her? Had the danger she'd felt all been in her imagination? It certainly seemed rather silly now to have thought herself a victim of white slavery. But she had been alone in a strange land, denied her freedom, and had known distinct unease, if not outright fear. And all because two men disliked each other!

They left the street lights behind and were driving through open country, but it was completely dark and Catriona could see nothing that wasn't illuminated by the car's headlamps: trees and the occasional mud brick house.

'How far is it?' she asked.

'Only a couple of miles. We turn off into the desert soon. Have you ever been to Egypt before?'

'No.'

'Then you're either going to love it or hate it; there are no half-measures where Egypt is concerned.'

'How long have you been out here?'

'On this excavation site, for three years, but I've spent a lot of time here during my career.'

'You discovered a new tomb, didn't you?'

'You've been doing some reading. Yes, nearly nine years ago. It wasn't a major find, though, and it had been robbed, of course, but there were some extremely good wall paintings.'

'You must have been young then,' Catriona remarked without thinking.

'Oh, yes, I was very young—then,' he agreed sardonically.

'I didn't mean to imply that you're no longer young, just that you must have been young to find a tomb,' she excused, afraid that he'd taken offence. Though he would have to be very vain to feel insulted by such a chance remark.

'I know what you meant. I was twenty-four—which some people seemed to think too immature to be put in charge of a dig and handle a find.'

So that was it. Catriona gave him a mental apology; obviously it was the criticism of his professionalism that rankled. Changing the subject, she said, 'How many people are there in your team?'

'Five principals: I'm the field director, and my deputy is our surveyor, Bryan Stone. Then we have a pottery expert, Harry Carson, who's in Cairo on leave at the moment, and a seed and plant man, Mike Pearson. The fifth man is Mohamed Shalaby, who's also the inspector from the Egyptian authorities.'

'No women?' Catriona asked with mixed feelings.

'There's Lamia, Mohamed's wife. She's not officially part of the team but she's supposed to run the house, make sure the servants do their work, that kind of thing.'

They had left the fertile area with its trees and fields, the road was no longer tarred, had become just an uneven, pot-holed track. Ahead she could see some lights

which turned out to be those of a small village of mud
houses. They drove through it, went on for another few
hundred yards, and then Lucas drove through an arched
gateway and pulled up in the courtyard of a house. Like
the Garden of the Nile, the house was two-storeyed, had
a gate and was surrounded by a wall. There the simi-
larity ended. There was no garden, no fountain playing,
no open door with welcoming servant, and, once inside,
definitely no air-conditioning or the faintest hint of
luxury. It was just a roughly made house, built to last
for the duration of the dig and nothing more. The furniture was old and shabby with no attempt at style. But
at least there was electric light, even if the bulbs didn't
possess shades.

Catriona stood in the hallway, looked about her, and
laughed again.

'Having second thoughts?' Lucas enquired as he
dropped her cases on the floor.

'Second, third and fourth,' Catriona admitted.

He grinned, and she liked it. 'I thought you might
have. Come and meet the others.'

He led her through a curtained doorway into a room
off to the left that evidently served as a communal sitting-
room. There was a television set in the corner but the
programme was in Arabic and only one man was
watching. Two other men were seated at a small table,
playing chess, and a woman sat on a worn settee, reading
a magazine. They all looked round when Lucas led her
in. For a long moment there was total silence and
Catriona felt rather like an exhibit at the zoo as their
eyes assessed her. It was one of the men at the table,
middle-aged and weather-beaten, who spoke first.

'So you found her.'

'Yes. She ended up at Omar Rafiq's house.' Lucas
turned to Catriona. 'This is Bryan Stone, the surveyor.
And this is Mike Pearson, our plant expert.'

The other chess-player stood up to shake hands. He was younger, around thirty, and there was an abstracted air about him, as if he was thinking of something else. 'Hello. Catriona Fenton, isn't it?'

'Yes. Hello.'

'And this is our Egyptian colleague, Mohamed.'

The man who had been watching television also stood up. '*Kayf haalak, tasharafna be-mearefatak,*' he said, bowing over her hand.

'"How do you do? Pleased to meet you",' Lucas translated.

Catriona smiled and came out with her only Arabic word. '*Shokran.* Thank you.'

'And this is Lamia, Mohamed's wife.'

Catriona had quite liked the look of Mohamed, but his wife was something else. She didn't bother to get up but reached up an indolent hand to let it be shaken. In her early thirties, she was dark-haired and attractive, but there was antagonism in her eyes. 'Hello.' Catriona smiled at her. 'I'm sorry I don't speak Arabic.'

The friendly overture was ignored as Lamia answered in perfect English. 'How *odd* that you got lost.' Making it sound as if she also thought it extremely stupid. 'How was Omar?'

'You know him?'

'Of course, or why should I ask?' Again as if she thought her a fool.

But Catriona could give as good as she got. 'He was very well,' she answered. Adding, 'How strange, when you know him so well, that he didn't send you his regards—or even mention your name.'

She thought she heard Lucas give a soft chuckle behind her but couldn't be sure. Lamia's eyes narrowed, but before she could speak Lucas said, 'We haven't eaten. Is there any food ready for us?'

'The cook had to stay on. I'll tell him you're here.'

Lucas let her go, not offering to do it for her. 'I'll show you your room,' he told Catriona.

He picked up her cases and she followed him up the stairs with her hand luggage. The roughly surfaced walls had been painted white, presumably throughout the building, but were now very dingy, and although there had been a couple of pictures on the walls of the sitting-room there was none elsewhere. On the first floor there were six rooms opening off the landing. Lucas pointed to one opposite the stairs. 'That's the bathroom. We all have to share it, I'm afraid. And water's scarce so you're only allowed two showers a week. Why are you grinning?'

' "From the sublime to the ridiculous",' Catriona quoted.

He had no comment to make about that. 'This is your room.' He opened a door to the right of the stairs, took her cases in and dropped them on the bed. 'See you downstairs in ten minutes.'

The room was clean and had the basic necessities: a bed, just a rail for her clothes, a wash-stand with old-fashioned jug and basin, a table with a light over it, and a chair. Catriona had seen pictures of prison cells that looked more comfortable. And it was so drab: white walls, no curtains at the high window, and a grey-coloured blanket on the bed. With a degree in art and design, it was the lack of colour that most offended her. And it would be the first thing that she would put right, she decided. If she was going to spend six months here, then there would have to be some colour in her life.

There was water, cold, in the jug, and the towels were clean. Catriona washed her face and hands, brushed her hair, added some lipstick, and went down to dine with Lucas Kane.

The dining-room had just one large table with half a dozen chairs set round it. But there was a tablecloth,

although it was already stained, and there was wine to
drink. The food, brought by a white-robed Egyptian boy,
was quite good. The conversation, though, wasn't.

'Did Omar tell you anything about me?' Lucas asked
her.

'Only that he knew you.'

'He didn't say anything about the dig—or the team?'

'Only that I would find the house most uncomfortable and I wouldn't like it here.'

Lucas's lips twisted into a grin at that, but he gave
the slightest nod of satisfaction, making Catriona wonder
just what Omar might have told her. Changing the
subject completely, he said, 'What experience have you
had?'

Dodgy ground. 'Didn't you have my CV? It's all in
there.'

'Yes, of course—but I'd like to know in detail.'

He would. With an inner sigh Catriona said, 'I have
an honours degree in art and design and did my thesis
on the influence of historic costume on modern fashion.
I then had a six-month placement in the textile conservation department of a museum, and after that——'

'They didn't offer to keep you on?' Lucas interrupted.

'No, they couldn't afford to. They were under-funded
and had to keep taking on new graduates for half-yearly
placements because that way they didn't have to pay very
much.'

He nodded, apparently satisfied. 'And after that...?'
he prompted.

'I worked in various aspects of the textile industry,
broadening my knowledge and experience.' She had
quoted verbatim from her CV because it was the best
way she knew of covering a catalogue of odd jobs that
she had been forced to take to earn a living. In the re-
cession there had just been no jobs going for a young,
ambitious girl with ideas of her own. And her looks

hadn't helped; often her qualifications had got her through to the interview stage, but museum curators and prospective employers had taken one glance at her delicate figure and fair beauty and refused to take her seriously, or else thought that she would soon marry and leave.

Once, she'd thought she'd really got the job she so wanted: designing costumes for an opera company who were launching an entirely new production. For a while all went well, but again the lack of finance had intervened, their sponsors had crashed and the new opera had been called off, making Catriona, along with a great many other people, unemployed yet again. For some time after that she'd had to work as a waitress, until she had found the job with a clothing company as a supervisor over a sweatshop of overworked immigrant women. This wasn't satisfactory, but at least she'd been working with clothes—until the day she had felt driven to complain about the women's pay and conditions and had been immediately dismissed. But how did you explain that to a man who had never been out of work, had been given his own excavation at twenty-four and had never looked back?

His grey eyes seemed to see into her mind. 'Elucidate,' he ordered shortly.

Catriona did so. She didn't lie, but she made the most of those jobs she'd had that she thought would be an advantage and glossed over those that didn't, and missed out the waitressing job completely.

She didn't fool him, she hadn't seriously thought she would, not once she'd met him and seen the kind of man he was. When she'd finished Lucas said, 'So beyond six months in a museum, two years ago, you have no practical experience of historic textiles, and probably none at all of ancient Egyptian.'

'Why did your last textile expert leave?' Catriona countered.

His eyebrows flickered. 'Personal reasons,' he answered dismissively.

But she wasn't to be put off. 'What personal reasons?'

'They need hardly concern you. She just found it necessary to leave.'

'She? It was a woman?'

'Aren't most textile experts nowadays?' And, before she could answer, 'Stop trying to change the subject. Have you or have you not any experience of ancient Egyptian textiles?'

'No. But I——'

'In other words you got the job under false pretences,' Lucas said harshly. He frowned angrily. 'I hate deceit. Can you give me one good reason why I shouldn't put you on the first plane back to England, *and* charge you for the fares we've wasted?'

'Yes,' Catriona answered promptly. 'You haven't got anyone else. And I *know* I can do this job.'

'Do you?' His eyes were on her earnest face and determined chin. 'If I thought that I could get hold of another expert quickly, I'd get rid of you tomorrow. But as it is...' He shrugged. 'I have no choice but to give you a try.'

'Thank you,' she said unsteadily.

'Keep your thanks,' he retorted brusquely. 'I'll give you a trial, but just remember that I'll be watching you like a hawk, so don't think you can cover up your mistakes or get away with anything. And first you're going to have to do a great deal of reading and studying before I let you near even the smallest thread of cloth on this site.'

'I was going to say that I've already been doing that, from the moment I knew there was a chance that I might come here.'

'Well, first thing tomorrow we're going to find out just what you do know.'

Overwhelmingly grateful that she wasn't about to be sent immediately back to England, Catriona gave a sigh of relief but didn't let it show. 'What time do we start?'

'Breakfast is at five-thirty.' He was watching her, expecting her to look dismayed, but Catriona merely nodded. 'Then we have a break around eleven, and afterwards work on at the site until about three. We come back here for a meal at four and usually spend the evening examining finds, repairing pottery, and doing basic conservation.'

'I see. Perhaps you could tell me something about the site you're working on.'

Lucas glanced at his watch. 'Tomorrow. I have some work to catch up on before I go to bed.' He pushed back his chair. 'You might as well go and unpack. Goodnight.'

Catriona had been waiting for the next course in the meal, but evidently that was it. 'Goodnight.'

She followed him out of the room and saw him go into a room next door, one she hadn't been into yet. Doing as he'd suggested, she went upstairs to unpack, hanging her clothes on the rail, and keeping her more personal possessions in the suitcases, which she pushed under the bed. The house was very quiet; presumably everybody went to bed early if they had to get up at five. Deciding to do the same, Catriona first went in search of the bathroom. It was like no bathroom she had ever seen before. To even call it that was to bestow a title it certainly didn't deserve. It was like calling a pigsty a porcine palace. There was no bath, and the shower was a joke. It was electric but the water was always tepid whichever setting you put it on, and came out in fits and starts, to be collected in a sort of baby's bath in which you stood, and was evidently saved and used again. Probably by the next person, Catriona thought with a

grimace. Remembering that she was only allowed two
showers a week and deciding that the need might be
greater tomorrow, Catriona went quickly back to her
room and washed herself as best she could.

Sitting up in bed, Catriona took out the textbooks
she'd brought with her and began to go through them
again, wanting to be as informed as possible before
tomorrow. At eleven o'clock she turned out the light,
but it took her a while to get to sleep, mostly because
she just wasn't tired, but also because the bed was hard
and lumpy and the room too warm.

Lying awake, she went over the extraordinary events
of the last twenty-four hours. She saw now how stupid
she had been to think that Omar's house could possibly
be the expedition headquarters; she ought to have insisted on Omar's being wakened and being taken back
to the airport at once. Well, it was too late now; she had
made a bad start with Lucas, and her lack of experience
hadn't helped either. But at least he'd let her stay, even
if it was only on a trial basis. She turned, trying to find
a comfortable spot, unable to resist comparing this room
with the opulence of the one she'd slept in last night.
Talk about rude awakenings—this must be the rudest
ever! She must be mad, she decided. Fancy turning down
Omar's plush palace for this!

Her thoughts drifted to the woman who had left the
dig team so suddenly. Had this been her room? Catriona
was rather intrigued by her. She herself had heard of
the job through an old college friend who worked at a
museum with a really good Egyptology department. The
friend had said that the textile expert had left at short
notice for family reasons, which could mean anything,
of course. But Catriona couldn't help but wonder what
had happened, especially now she'd learnt the previous
expert had been a woman. Was it anything to do with
Lucas? Perhaps the woman hadn't been able to stand

his overbearing behaviour. It was even possible that she'd fallen for him and been snubbed. Unlikely, although there was definitely something attractive about Lucas: his lean good-looks, and the sort of rough arrogance that a woman could fall for if she wasn't careful.

Lying on the bumpy pillow, Catriona wondered what Lucas would be like as a lover. He'd be experienced, she guessed, physically expert as far as the sex part of it went. But if a woman wanted more, if she fell in love with him and looked for the same feelings from him... Catriona just couldn't see it. Lucas definitely looked the love 'em and leave 'em type. She could imagine him becoming cynically amused and hurtfully mocking if some poor female tried to get really close to him. A good enough reason for the last textile expert to have left so precipitately.

Her alarm clock had been set for five o'clock, but it seemed that she had only just got to sleep when its strident tone shattered the stillness. For a few minutes Catriona was too sleepy to think where she was, but then remembered and sat up with a jerk. Today was going to be a testing time, in more ways than one. Quickly she got up, stood naked in front of the basin to wash herself in the now tepid water, dressed in shirt and trousers and plaited her hair into its practical pleat. No make-up today, she decided; she wanted to look as efficient and intellectual as possible—which, she'd found, in a man's eyes seemed to require her also to look as unfeminine as possible. Which wasn't easy; no matter how she tried, Catriona had never succeeded in looking anything less than classy.

Lamia didn't put in an appearance at breakfast but all the rest of the team were there, although nobody talked very much. Lucas's eyes flicked over her and he nodded when she said good morning, but apart from that he didn't speak. As soon as they'd finished, everyone

piled into the Land Rover to drive the short distance to
the site. Outside, the sun was still low and it was beautifully cool. There were no trees and no other houses near
by, just the long spread of the desert, broken by hills,
but on the far horizon the land rose into mountains,
jaggedly outlined against the rising sun. It was very still,
very beautiful. Catriona paused to stand and stare, could
happily have stayed for longer, but Lucas started the
engine and she had to run and jump in beside Mohamed.

She was put in Bryan Stone's charge. He took over
the Land Rover and drove her round the excavation,
explaining that it was a settlement site of about 1400
BC. It covered a wider area than she expected. There
were the remains of temples and palaces, and large resi-
dential quarters, and Bryan told her there were tombs
built into the distant desert cliffs. 'We're concentrating
on the suburb to the north,' he told her. 'There's a group
of very large houses in their own estates, and also a
number of smaller houses surrounding them.'

'What about the rest of the city?'

'Other teams, from various countries, are working on
other sites, but they mainly only work in the winter when
it's cooler. The French are still here, but most of the
others have gone home and won't be back till October
or November.'

'So how come our team is still working?'

Bryan gave a short laugh. 'It's Lucas; he wants to get
the job done.'

'And move on to something else?'

'Partly that, but mostly because he's eager to find all
there is to find. He's obsessed by everything that's hidden
under the sand, and can't wait to discover its secrets.'

A strong word to describe a man's interest, his career,
but there had been many men in the past who had shared
the obsession, and had found the treasure of King
Tutankhamun in the process. The buried treasure syn-

drome. A bug that, once caught, would, Catriona
guessed, be almost impossible to shake off. And Lucas
would have caught it early by finding a tomb when still
so young.

'I'll take you back to where we're working,' Bryan
told her.

About a dozen workers from the nearby village had
arrived, tramping across the desert on foot, and were
gathered round Lucas as he told them where to work.
He sent two men off with Bryan, then told two others
and Catriona to follow him.

'This is the courtyard of one of the houses,' he
explained when they came to a certain part of the ruins.
'I want you to work along this wall, carefully brushing
away the sand and sifting through it. When you've filled
up one of these baskets, Gamal here will take it and dump
it out of the way.'

'What if I find anything?' Catriona asked, keeping
any nervousness out of her voice.

'Then log it in this book and put it carefully into a
finds tray. I'll look at it when we have our break. OK?'

'Fine,' Catriona returned, feeling anything but.

Lucas walked away. Catriona watched him go, his
broad figure casting a long shadow on the sand, then
got down on her knees and started work. The two natives
sat and watched. She had been on digs before, of course,
but never in soft sand. Working from the corner, she
steadily brushed and sifted along a three-foot stretch.
She found a few stones that looked like ordinary stones
rather than a hieroglyph that would, in one glorious clue,
solve the hidden puzzle of the whole site. But, fearful
of making a mistake, she showed them to Gamal, raising
her eyebrows. He gave them a cursory glance, tossed
them in the basket, and went back to watching her work.

Then she brushed sand from another stone which she
loosened, examined and tossed aside. She was about to

go on when she noticed a scrap of colour under where it had rested. For a moment she froze with excitement, then very, very carefully began to brush the sand away. It was a piece of cloth, terribly faded, but it was clear that it had once been blue. Hardly daring to breathe in case it fell to pieces, Catriona carefully eased it free. Wow! she thought. I've actually found something on my very first day.

Taking a soft, fine brush from her work bag, she gently cleaned the piece of cloth, her heart thudding in nervous excitement. Taking a closer look, she frowned and touched it with her fingertip, finding the texture coarse and hard. Picking up the finds tray that Lucas had left with her, she carefully put it inside and wrote in the log-book. Then went on with her task.

Gamal and the boy had carried away several baskets of sand by the time the whistle blew for break. It had got much hotter and she had put on an old baseball cap to shield her eyes. Thankfully Catriona got to her feet and walked over to where the others were gathered under a shelter of woven palm fronds. Lucas had a table where he could note down any finds and mark them on his map of the site. The boy from the house had brought a cool-box with several bottles of cold mineral water. He offered Catriona a plastic cup and filled it for her. She drank deeply, already hot and sweating.

The others were standing around, drinking, not talking much, and no one was looking at her. Catriona merely asked for another cup of water, trying to keep all emotion out of her face, determined not to be the first to speak.

'Anybody find anything?' Lucas asked. The others shook their heads. 'How about you, Catriona?' he said, his voice casual.

She let the excitement show. 'As a matter of fact I did find something.'

'You did? Great! What was it?'

'Here.' She took the finds tray carefully over to him. 'It's a piece of cloth,' she said in reverential tones.

Lucas picked it from the tray with a pair of tweezers and looked at it intently. 'Any idea what it could be?'

'As a matter of fact I have,' she said in breathless excitement.

'Really? What?' They were all crowding eagerly round her now.

'Well—it will really rewrite the history books! You see, this small scrap of cloth actually proves——' she paused for effect '—that they were using *denim* in 1400 BC. And I think this is actually a scrap from a pair of Tutankhamun's jeans!'

There was a roar of laughter as they realised they'd been had, and even Lucas grinned and nodded. He had planted the piece of cloth for her to find, expecting to fool her, but she had neatly turned the tables on him, and Catriona rather thought she had won that round.

CHAPTER THREE

CATRIONA was very glad when they finally broke up that day. Since the first break she had been working in the shade, but even so felt terribly hot and dry. She hadn't found anything interesting, which hadn't surprised her; as soon as she'd realised the trick that had been played on her she'd known that Lucas wouldn't trust her with any responsibility until she'd proved herself. Which she intended to do just as soon as possible—or as soon as Lucas would allow her to, she thought wryly.

They were mostly silent as they drove back, all of them tired and hungry. The jug in Catriona's room had been filled with water again, but if it had been cool at all it was now tepid. Trying to push thoughts of the bathroom in Omar's house out of her mind, she stripped off her clothes and washed herself, letting the water trickle down over her hot flesh. It didn't cool her but it made her feel better. Even though she'd been wearing the hat her hair seemed full of sand, and had to be brushed vigorously, which made her hot again. Tomorrow she'd do it the other way round. Finding a skirt and blouse, she changed into them, added some make-up, and went downstairs for the main meal of the day.

Lamia wasn't there, so the talk was all of the site and an interesting wall that the workmen had started to uncover. Catriona sat and listened, eager to learn as much as she could. Lucas glanced at her from time to time and she began to wonder whether he expected her to join in the conversation, but she had so little experience of this field and period that she judged it better to keep quiet rather than make a fool of herself. But she sighed inwardly, guessing that she was sinking ever lower in his estimation.

After the meal Lucas went off to his office while the rest of them went to the sitting-room. Even here they weren't cut off from the dig, though, because there was a large-scale map of the site pinned on the wall. Mohamed switched on the television but Bryan and Mike sat down in armchairs to read the packet of English newspapers that had been delivered while they were at the dig. Catriona went over to study the map, relating it to what she'd seen that morning.

She was still standing in front of it when Lucas came in ten minutes later. Crossing to her side, he said, 'Have you found out where you were yet?'

'Yes. Here.' She pointed to the corner where the scrap of denim had been planted.

'At least you can read a map.'

'I can also read that you excavated that area over six months ago,' Catriona said tartly. 'My whole day has been wasted.'

'Not if it taught you how to work in the sand and what to look for.'

'And tomorrow?' she asked, unable to keep the sharpness out of her voice. 'Am I going to "practise" again?'

His eyes narrowing, Lucas said, 'Does that bother you?'

Managing to hold her angry disappointment in check, she shrugged. 'You're paying for my time, so if you——' The door had opened behind them. Catriona glanced round and saw that Lamia had come into the room. But it was the other girl's appearance that made her break off in surprise. Lamia had obviously been to the hairdresser and had her hair done in a different style, swept back from her face and fastened with a bow at

the nape. She wore a tight-fitting dress in deep red silk
with black accessories and was heavily made-up, her
black-outlined eyes and full lips reminding Catriona of
an ancient Egyptian wall painting. She looked mature
and sophisticated, and completely out of place in this
primitive house.

The heads of all the men, including her husband's,
turned towards her, but Catriona noticed that it wasn't
to Mohamed but to Lucas that Lamia looked first.

Catriona swiftly looked at him herself, interested to
see his reaction. His eyes swept over Lamia but, beyond
a slightly sardonic curl of the lip, Lucas's expression
didn't change and she was none the wiser.

'Going somewhere special, Lamia?' Lucas asked, his
eyes on the other girl.

'I have *been* to Luxor,' Lamia answered, her chin
coming up.

'Oh, I see. Been shopping, I suppose.' Adding, before
she could answer, 'Find anything interesting?'

He seemed to emphasise the last word and Catriona
thought Lamia flushed a little, but it was hard to tell
under all that make-up. 'I bought one or two things,
yes. Mohamed needed some new shirts.'

'How very commendable of you to think of him.'

There was a slight but definite note of sarcasm in
Lucas's tone, and Catriona was sure now that there was
some kind of intrigue here. Mohamed, though, seemed
completely unaware of it. After greeting his wife he had
turned back to the television, apparently intent on
watching the news. Bryan and Mike, too, had gone back
to their newspapers, but Catriona was sure that they were
still listening.

'And did you order the supplies we need while you
were so busily doing your shopping?' Lucas asked.

'Of course. They will be delivered next week.'

'All of them?'

Lamia looked a little annoyed. 'So they said.'

'Did you actually check that they had the stuff in stock—check personally?'

The other woman's annoyance deepened. 'Do you expect me to look along the shelves of a warehouse in all the dust and dirt? To count shovels and bags of flour?'

'Yes, Lamia, I do. And you know full well I do. You're supposed to be in charge of supplies. If everything isn't counted and checked we'll get ripped off, as we have done in the past. And we can't afford it.' Lucas hadn't raised his voice, in fact he spoke almost on a conversational level, but there was menace in his tone as he said, 'If you can't be trusted to make sure we get the correct supplies then there's no place for you here. Do you understand?'

Lamia gave him a sulky look, her lower lip pouting. 'The supplies will all be here. Have I not said so?' And, picking up her handbag, she walked angrily from the room.

Turning back to the map as if the unpleasant little incident had never taken place, Lucas said, 'When I'm satisfied that you know what you're looking for, then, and only then, will I let you loose on a part of the dig that we haven't yet excavated. Tomorrow you can work with Mike. Here.' He stabbed his finger at a spot about a hundred yards from where she'd been that day. 'There was a garden with a pool here once and it's yielding some interesting plant finds.' He turned to face her. 'But now I'd like you to come with me.'

Catriona followed him to the room which she'd supposed was his office. It had a heavy wooden door which Lucas unlocked with a key attached to a chain on his belt. The room was lined with metal shelving and there was a large work table in the middle with several fluorescent light tubes hanging over it.

'This is our finds room and where we do primary conservation work,' he told her. 'Anything that needs a lot of work goes to a museum workshop.'

'What about anything precious?' Catriona couldn't resist asking.

Lucas gave a short laugh. 'I suppose by "precious" you mean gold or jewellery. Why is it that's the first thing people ever think about where a dig is concerned—especially females? This is a town, not a tomb, woman. The most we're likely to find are interesting household artefacts—which are equally *precious* in the eyes of the archeologist.'

'But hardly to be compared with something as exciting as the Tutankhamun treasure, surely?'

'Have you seen it?'

'Yes, when it was on exhibition in London.'

'That was ages ago. I'll try and arrange for you to go and see it in the museum in Cairo.'

'Thank you,' Catriona said in pleased surprise.

Spoiling it, Lucas said, 'With your lack of experience it will give you an opportunity to study some of the textile finds they have there. Everything from King Tut's tunic down to a laundry pile of loincloths, and a model of a weaver's shop. And for God's sake put all thoughts of finding a tomb full of treasure out of your head. You can learn far more from a workmen's village than you can from a tomb.'

'Really?' Catriona said disbelievingly. 'I thought the mummified bodies themselves were the most interesting and gave the most information about the people and their way of life.'

'Where did you read that? You're talking like a textbook.'

'I have been boning-up on the subject,' Catriona admitted.

'Reading bears no comparison with actual hands-on experience,' Lucas said dismissively. 'Especially with textiles.'

Feeling that she couldn't win, Catriona was goaded into saying, 'Studying and revising a subject must always help.'

'Really? All right, let's see what you do know.' He gestured to a chair by the table. 'Sit down there.'

Catriona did so in some dismay, wondering what she'd talked herself into. She watched as Lucas went over to the shelves and selected several trays. He seemed to know exactly which ones to pick, and she suddenly realised that she had been deliberately manipulated into this test, that he'd intended it all along. But it was clever of him to make her think it was her own fault.

Bringing the trays over, Lucas put them on the table, then set the first one in front of her. Sitting down beside her, he said, 'OK, what can you tell me about that piece of cloth there?' And he pointed with a long finger at a small, transparent plastic bag in the tray.

It wasn't the first time that a tutor or someone similar had sat beside her and asked her questions. Beyond a natural wish not to make a mistake it had never bothered her before, but now Catriona found it difficult to give the items the intense concentration they needed. She was aware of Lucas watching her, of his closeness. He must have showered and shaved after they got back, because she caught the tang of his aftershave, clean and woody. His physical presence, too, was strong, because he was so big, so broad-shouldered and masculine.

Abruptly, some subconscious instinct suddenly making her afraid of her own senses, Catriona's brain jerked into gear and she became aware only of the task he'd set her. She was allowed to take the scrap from the bag with tweezers, to examine it under a microscope, frowned with concentration, answered. Was given another artefact and went through the procedure again. And again and again. Because the site was around 1300 BC Catriona had concentrated her recent study on that period, but Lucas had slipped in a couple of items from other periods, which had thrown her for a while until she'd realised. She'd had to answer as best she could and wasn't at all sure that she'd been right.

A couple of hours later they finished the last tray and Lucas sat back. Catriona gave an inner sigh of relief and let her shoulders sag as she relaxed the inner tension. Picking up the trays, Lucas carefully put them back in their correct places. She waited for him to speak, to tell her how she'd done, but when he didn't she said impatiently, 'Well, have I passed the test you set me?'

'I thought you merely wished to show me that study was equal to experience.'

'No, that was what *you* wanted me to think. You had this test in mind all along. Why else did you bring me in here?'

Coming over, he half sat on the edge of the table. 'It seems you can think as well as study.'

'It didn't take much working out.'

'Perhaps not.' He paused, his eyes on her face, then said, 'You did OK, but your knowledge isn't deep enough. One of the pieces of cloth I showed you had a small mark on it. You noticed the mark but didn't realise that it could have been put there deliberately as a laundry mark.' Catriona gasped in surprise, and he nodded. 'Oh, yes, even the Egyptians had laundries and marks. An experienced expert would have realised what it was or what it might be. You're good, Catriona, but you're not good enough—not yet.'

Her heart sank as she waited for him to tell her that he would replace her as soon as he could. 'Not—yet?' she repeated hollowly.

'No. So I've decided to give you a crash course in everything you need to know. I'll provide you with the necessary books and arrange for you to talk to a textile expert who knows the subject like the back of his hand—better probably. Then, after two or three weeks of intensive work—in your leisure time, of course—maybe you'll be of some use to me.'

'Thank you,' Catriona said unsteadily. 'I'm—I'm very grateful.'

'So you should be,' Lucas answered, straightening up. 'I just hope I don't come to regret it.'

Catriona went up to bed around nine, which felt ridiculously early, but she fell asleep immediately, tired out by the tensions of the day. A combination of feeling hot and the lumpy pillow and mattress woke her in the night. At first she determinedly closed her eyes and tried to go to sleep again, but after a while got up and bathed her hot skin with what was left of the water. The window in the room wasn't very large but it might let in some cooler air. Catriona reached up to push it open but found that the darn thing was stuck. Pulling up the chair, she stood on it and pushed at the frame but it hardly moved. She stopped to rest, finding the least exertion only made her hotter, and leaned with her arms on the sill, looking out.

It was a beautiful starlit night, the sand of the desert acting almost like a mirror to reflect the moonlight. A movement inside the compound caught her eye and she saw the tall figure of a man walk into sight, his shadow long behind him. Catriona thought it was Lucas but he had his back towards her and the glass pane was dirty so she couldn't be sure. She rubbed at it with her hand but it didn't make much difference. The man walked the length of the compound, then turned and walked back. Now the moonlight was on his face. She had been right, it was Lucas. He retraced his footsteps, his head bent, as if he had something on his mind. But then he disappeared into the shadows again and she guessed that he had entered the house.

Getting back into bed, Catriona thought about Lucas, wondered why he wasn't married, what he'd been thinking about down there in the moonlight. She pondered over him for quite some time, but told herself it was merely to keep her mind off the lumpy bed, until she eventually fell asleep again.

The next morning she went with Mike to the garden pool. He was even more taciturn in the mornings and became impatient when she asked questions. 'Just watch,' he told her tersely. She obeyed, and was amazed at his patience as he recorded every plant that grew in the area, just in case there was anything at all unusual. After a couple of hours he became more sociable and let her work on her own. She didn't find anything but, after their break, there was some excitement as Lucas, who was working alone on a small house, unearthed a strange model figure, the upper half of a man. He cleaned it off and showed it to them back at the house at the end of the day.

The others had never seen anything like it before but Lucas said, 'It's similar to a figure they've got in the museum. I think it may be part of a magician's bag of tricks.'

'A magician?' Catriona queried. 'You mean an entertainer?'

'Possibly more of a witch-doctor. Which makes this piece quite rare, I think.'

They were all pleased with the find and talked about it, and its implications, all through dinner. Afterwards Catriona went into the sitting-room with the others but Lucas brought in a pile of books and put them down in front of her. 'Here's your first batch of reading,' he told her. 'And here's a list of the order they should be read in.'

The implication was that she should start at once, and Catriona was willing enough. She carried the books over to a table by the window, found a notepad and pen, and set to work.

Lamia had been at dinner with them and afterwards went to her room for a short while, but then came into the sitting-room for coffee. The men, Mohamed among them, went into the finds room to take photographs of the figure which they were going to send to the museum to be identified. Lamia stayed behind and turned on the television, rather loudly, then glanced over at Catriona. But Catriona had shared a flat with several other girls when she was at college and was used to having to study with noise going on around her, so took no notice. She knew that it was on, though, and guessed that the other woman had done it merely to annoy her.

When she didn't get any reaction, Lamia turned up the volume. Already concentrating intensely, to the exclusion of all else, Catriona merely put her fingers over her ears and went on reading.

'What the hell's going on here?' Lucas strode into the room, took in the situation at a glance, walked over to the television set and switched it off.

'I was watching that,' Lamia said indignantly. 'I have a right to watch it if I want to.'

'You know that Catriona is trying to study.'

'Then let her do it somewhere else.'

Crossing over to Catriona, Lucas said her name, but when she took no notice put his hand on her shoulder. She felt that all right. Startled, she looked up and saw him, then glanced at Lamia's angry face.

'Why don't you go and study somewhere where you won't be disturbed by the television?' Lucas suggested.

'It doesn't bother me; I can shut it out.'

'Very likely,' he said drily. 'But it seems to bother
Lamia. And she's right; this is supposed to be a leisure
room where she can watch the goggle box.'

'I'm not stopping her.'

Lucas frowned. 'Don't argue about it, girl, just find
somewhere else.'

Catriona didn't much like being called that. It made
her say obstinately, 'I don't care how loud she has it,
and I'm quite happy here, thanks.'

He gave a sharp sigh of exasperation. 'Women! Just
go and work in your room, will you?'

Annoyed, Catriona gathered up her books, but Lucas
didn't wait to watch her, he just went out again. Lamia
smiled triumphantly and as Catriona went to the door
said, 'That's right. Go up to your room like a good little
girl.'

Turning at the door, Catriona raised her voice to say
loudly, 'I'm so sorry, Lamia, I should have realised that
at your age you must be hard of hearing,' and went
quickly out of the room.

Her own room was hot and uncomfortable. After a
while she went in search of the servant boy and got him
to force her window open. It made her a bit cooler but
not much and she doubted if it would ever shut again.
But at least that night the room was cooler and she slept
better, only waking to shake lumps out of the pillow, to
knock away a fly that kept buzzing round her, to have
a drink of water, and to change position half a dozen
times. On the whole not a bad night, as nights in Egypt
seemed to go.

When she got up the next morning she discovered that
it hadn't been a fly but a whole family of mosquitoes
who'd been having a banquet while she was asleep. She
was covered in bites—and they itched! She'd decided to
put on shorts today, as the men did, but instead put on
jeans and a long-sleeved blouse, to stop herself from

scratching as much as to hide the bites. It wasn't successful, though; the material rubbing against the bites made them itch more than ever. Mike of course didn't notice; he seldom seemed to notice anything much apart from his precious plants, but when Lucas came over to see how they were getting on he saw the look on her face as she rubbed her arm.

'Sunburn?' he asked without sympathy.

'No, mosquito bites.'

'Are you taking your malaria tablets?'

'Yes, of course.'

'Then make sure you keep the net over you at night.'

Catriona gave him a puzzled look. 'What net?'

Lucas had been going to turn away but he swung back to face her. 'A mosquito net. Hasn't Lamia put one in your room?'

'No,' Catriona said feelingly. 'She hasn't.'

'I'll tell her tonight.'

'Don't worry—I'll tell her myself. Why does she dislike me?' she asked in bewilderment. 'What has she got against me?'

Lucas shrugged, uninterested. 'How should I know how women's minds work, why they take a dislike to each other?'

'I'm willing enough to be friends,' she protested.

'I hardly think Lamia is interested in having a *girl*friend,' Lucas remarked, his mouth twisting in amusement.

He walked away then, leaving Catriona looking after him as she scratched at another bite. A fat lot of sympathy for them she'd got from Lucas. Anger filled her as she thought that this torment could have been avoided if it hadn't been for Lamia. Catriona was fast coming to lose patience with her and her tricks.

Turning to Mike, she said abruptly, 'Do *you* know why Lamia dislikes me?'

For a minute he looked completely thrown, as if he wasn't used to having his opinion asked on anything except plants. He cleared his throat and hesitated, hesitated again, before saying, 'She likes to have things her own way.'

'Really? In what way?' Catriona said encouragingly.

'I think she likes to be the centre of attention,' Mike offered.

Catriona could understand that; she rather thought it was why Lamia dolled herself up so much. 'But she is, isn't she?'

Mike shook his head, sure of his answer this time. 'Not now you're here.'

'But the last textile expert was a woman.'

'Yes, but she was older and—and not so attractive,' he said with acute embarrassment.

'Oh, I see. Thank you.' She paused, wondering if it would be any use, but then said in a casual voice that any man with experience of women would have been wary of, 'Mike, just why did the last woman leave?'

Mike immediately flushed and looked away. 'I've—er—no idea.'

'None at all?'

'No. No, none.'

'When I heard about this job I was told she'd left for—personal reasons.'

'Yes, that's right.'

'Family reasons,' Catriona pursued mercilessly.

Poor Mike put a hand up to his collar as if to loosen a non-existent tie. 'Er—yes, I suppose so.'

Catriona gave him a pleading look, her hazel eyes opening wide. It was a look that quite a few men had been unable to resist in the past. 'Won't you tell me, Mike? I won't tell anyone, I promise. You see, it's just that I don't want to make the same mistake she did.'

'I—I don't really know. I'm not sure.'

'But you do know *something*?'

He nodded unhappily. 'Elaine—that was her name, Elaine—she—she had to leave. You see, she—er—slipped up.'

'You mean Lucas threw her out because she messed up a find or something?' Catriona guessed, having unwelcome visions of doing the same thing.

But Mike said, 'No, nothing like that. She got into trouble.'

Catriona frowned, then light dawned as she recognised the dated expression. 'You mean she got pregnant?' she exclaimed.

Making shushing movements with his hands, Mike nodded. 'Yes.'

'Who by? Who was the father?'

But Mike shook his head and closed his lips into an obstinate line. 'I don't know for sure and I'm not going to say who I suspect. It wouldn't be fair.'

She could probably have wheedled it out of him but Catriona knew it would upset him, so she smiled warmly and said, 'No, it wouldn't. But thanks for telling me, Mike; I couldn't help but wonder.'

'I suppose not.' He hesitated, then said stumblingly, 'You'll be careful, won't you, Catriona? You seem so frail. It isn't easy for girls in Egypt. You—*you* won't make a mistake, will you?'

'No,' Catriona assured him, hoping she'd have more sense. Although out here in the desert, in close association with lonely men by day and by night for months on end, it was hardly any wonder that an affair had developed. An affair with a man who had refused to stand by this Elaine, from the way it sounded. Catriona was interested in people and was intrigued to know who the man could have been. Definitely not Mike, she decided, or he would never have told her. Bryan Stone, the surveyor, was a possibility. He was older of course, but then Mike had said that Elaine was older, which would make her at least thirty. And Catriona had had enough passes made at her by men older than Bryan to know that men didn't lose their libido with middle age—far from it. Then of course there was Lucas. A mental awareness of his virile masculinity filled her senses. Yes, any woman, of any age, might well fall in love with him. A fatal action that, if it wasn't reciprocated, she thought would bring only pain and grief.

Lucas drove off in the car during the afternoon and Lamia, too, was out when they got back to the house after work, so Catriona went in search of a mosquito net and found several of them tucked away in a cupboard. The boy, Aly, fixed it up for her and also produced an old-fashioned fly-spray full of insect repellent which he energetically sprayed all over the room, including her bed. The stuff smelt terrible and repelled Catriona as much as the mosquitoes. It was impossible to work in that atmosphere, so she rather defiantly carried her books down to the sitting-room.

She needn't have worried; both Lucas and Lamia were out the whole evening and the other men spent most of the evening in the finds room where they were repairing some pottery. They were still there when Catriona went up to bed, her eyes heavy with tiredness.

Tonight it wasn't the mosquitoes but the bites they'd left behind that kept her awake. Catriona tried lying absolutely still, tried not to scratch, even tried mind over matter until her head ached, but nothing worked. The heat in the room, inflaming her skin, seemed to exacerbate the irritation the bites caused and drove her crazy. Unable to stand it any longer, Catriona was driven to action; if she didn't do something she'd go mad! The water in her bowl was used up and she'd already had her two showers for the week, but she knew that a shower was the only way she was going to get cool. She had been wearing nothing in bed, but now she pulled on a long T-shirt that came halfway down to her knees and slipped out to the bathroom.

The water was tepid again, not even cool, but to Catriona's feverish body it felt absolutely heavenly, like standing outside in a tropical rainstorm. She turned her face up to it and let it flow through her hair and on down her body. Gorgeous! Fantastic! Lifting her hair, Catriona turned so that the water could cool her neck and cascade down her back. Her eyes were closed and she was lost in sensual pleasure. The water stopped suddenly. She gave a little whimper of disappointment, thinking that it must have run out. She opened her eyes and found herself looking over the door—straight at Lucas!

She nearly jumped out of her skin with surprise, then yelled, 'Get out of here!'

'No, *you* get out,' he shot back. 'I guessed you'd soon be sneaking in here for a shower you weren't entitled to.'

'I'm borrowing against next week.'

'Like hell. Just come on out,' Lucas ordered.

Catriona clung to the doors in case he wrenched them open. 'I'm not moving until you get out of here, you— you peeping Tom!' she exclaimed angrily.

He laughed. 'Is that what you think? You needn't worry—when you've seen one you've seen 'em all!' But he added, 'I'll wait outside. Make it fast.'

As she hadn't brought a towel with her, Catriona didn't have any excuse not to. She squeezed the water out of her hair and pulled the T-shirt back on, but it was thin and clung to her, becoming almost transparent over her damp breasts and the soft roundness of her hips and stomach. The shower was in the 'OFF' position and she realised that Lucas must have reached past her to turn the knob while she'd had her eyes shut. So how long had he been there and how much had he seen? His last remark, uttered so disparagingly, was the opposite of reassuring.

So Catriona came out of the bathroom warily, her eyes searching his face for the least sign of concupiscence.

Lucas was standing in a pool of light, his hands on his hips, only impatience in his face. 'You know darn well you've had your quota of showers. It's unfair on the rest of us if you take more.'

Lamia was always so clean and cool-looking that Catriona was sure she must have as many showers as she felt like when they were all at the dig and there was no one to see her, but thought that the middle of the night was hardly the time to point this out. If he didn't know it already. Which she guessed he did; Lucas seemed to be on the ball where the team was concerned. But maybe he allowed Lamia special privileges. Pushing that strangely unwelcome thought aside, Catriona said evenly, 'I wouldn't have had a shower unless I was desperate. My room is like an oven and the mosquito bites were driving me mad. I figured it was the only way I could cool off enough to get to sleep. I hardly think you want me dropping from tiredness, do you?'

He looked at her assessingly for a moment, then said, 'Have you got many bites?'

'Yes, loads,' she answered feelingly.

'You'd better go to your room.'

Surprised that she'd got off so lightly, Catriona hurried to obey him, pulling the door shut behind her. Immediately the hot air struck her but she slipped quickly under the mosquito net and sat on the bed, running her fingers through her hair to dry it a little.

The light snapped on and Lucas was there again. Lifting the net, he sat on the bed beside her. Catriona stared, open-mouthed with astonishment at his effrontery.

But he said in an almost businesslike tone, 'I've brought some stuff to ease the bites. Where are they?' Then, impatiently, 'Stop gaping at me, Catriona. Anyone would think you'd never had a man in your bedroom before. Now, where are these bites?'

'They're all over,' she answered, too surprised to think carefully before she spoke.

'Well, I'll do the ones you can't reach for you, but I'm afraid you'll have to do the rest yourself,' he said mockingly. 'You'd better lie down on your front.'

She threw him a look of strong indignation, but was so overwhelmed with gratitude at the thought of the easing of this torture that she willingly did as he suggested. He did her legs and then the backs of her arms and the back of her neck. She expected his hands to be hard and rough but they were quite soft and surprisingly gentle, and the ointment so cooling that she almost purred.

'Anywhere else?' Lucas asked.

She sat up and hesitated. 'I do have some on my back.'

'OK, take that thing off and I'll do them.'

'Right. Er...' She looked at him.

Raising his eyebrows in a look of long-suffering, Lucas shrugged and turned his back while she wriggled under the sheet, pulled off the still damp shirt, and decorously covered her front.

'OK, you can turn round.'

He did so, and gave an exclamation. 'You must have about a hundred bites. How on earth did the mosquitoes get under your nightclothes?'

'I wasn't wearing any.'

'And you had kicked the bedcovers off too, I suppose.'

'It's baking hot in here, Lucas. I couldn't sleep.'

'Some people never learn.' But his fingers were incredibly gentle as he worked the ointment into the bites. It took a while and he didn't seem to hurry. Catriona tried to feel impersonal but it was almost impossible. She couldn't remember the last time a man had touched her so intimately without it being a precursor to sex, a deliberate attempt to arouse her senses. It must have been her father, rubbing oil into her back on the last holiday when they had all been together before her parents had split up. Such a long time ago now, almost twelve years. Nothing had been the same after he'd gone, her mother had become bitter and her brother wild.

Catriona gave a long, low sigh and Lucas said, 'What are you thinking about?' his voice soft.

'My father,' she answered honestly.

'Good grief!' His movements became quicker and it seemed only a short time later when he said, 'That's your back done. How about your behind?'

'I can manage that, thanks,' she said hastily.

'Suit yourself.' Lucas stood up and gave her the tube of ointment. 'Don't let yourself get in this state again.'

'No, I won't. I'll be up in time for work tomorrow.'

He grinned. 'No need. It's Friday. The religious holy day here in Egypt, when the men don't work. So you can have a lie-in.'

'Really? Great!'

'Yes—till seven. Then I've arranged for you to go over to the site the French are working on. They have an Egyptian textile expert who's agreed to help you.'

For a moment there she'd actually thought she was going to get a day off. With a small smile Catriona said, 'I'll be glad to learn from him. Thanks for fixing it up.' He turned to go and she said, 'And Lucas—thanks for the—the first-aid treatment. It's helping a lot.'

He nodded but raised a warning finger. 'Don't think I'm going to let you get away with that shower. You miss one out just as soon as those bites have cleared up, understand?'

'Yes. Thanks.'

'Goodnight.'

He carefully lifted up the net and ducked under it, tucked it in again before going to the doorway. For a moment she looked at him through the gauzy material, his outline blurred by it. Is this how the world looks to a bride looking through her veil? Catriona wondered fancifully. Does the world have this misty look and the bridegroom his hard edges softened? Is everything out of focus for a while until the knot is tied and you're transferred from father to husband, from maiden to wife? Then you lift the veil and all is reality again.

Lucas pushed open the door and went out. As he did so she heard a step out on the landing and then Lamia's laugh, mocking and cruel, 'Why, Lucas, leaving so soon? You obviously didn't find very much to—amuse you. She's obviously as bad as the other one. These English girls are all the same.' And again her laugh rang out through the silent house.

Catriona was glad of the lie-in because it had taken a while to go to sleep even though the bites were no longer plaguing her. Lamia was becoming a pain. The other girl had taken an immediate dislike to her and seemed to be intent on making life as difficult as possible. Maybe she was even out to get rid of her; although what good that would do, Catriona couldn't imagine. Lucas would only engage another textile expert, most of whom were women, so another would come out and Lamia would probably go through the whole process again. Except that Catriona was determined to make a go of this job and certainly wasn't going to be pushed out of it because of Lamia's petty jealousy. Whatever Lamia could dish out, she could take. Catriona was dismally aware, though, that by tomorrow morning the whole team would have been told that Lucas had been in her room.

She knew, immediately she entered the dining-room for breakfast, that she'd been right. Bryan gave her a quick, contemplative glance, then turned his head away, while the look Mohamed threw her was definitely contemptuous. Mike wouldn't even look at her, keeping his eyes on his plate as he ate. Lucas was there, too, but had his back to her so she couldn't see his reaction.

Going to her seat, Catriona said, 'Good morning,' in a determinedly bright voice and smiled at Aly as he put a plate of scrambled eggs in front of her.

As soon as she sat down, Lamia gave her a dazzling smile, all white teeth and full lips painted deep red, which was almost enough to put Catriona off her eggs. 'Good morning, Catriona. I hope you slept well—eventually?'

'Yes, I did—eventually,' Catriona agreed.

Everyone else immediately glanced surreptitiously at Lucas, but he went on placidly eating, and reading a letter he'd received, apparently unaware of the charged atmosphere.

Raising her voice just a little, Catriona said, 'Did you have a pleasant evening last night, Lamia?'

'Yes, I did. I spent the evening in Luxor with friends,' the older girl felt compelled to add.

'Really? Where did you go?' Catriona asked, pretending a polite interest.

'To a bridge party.'

'How clever. I wish I could play bridge. Perhaps you would teach me?'

Lamia waved a disinterested hand. 'There would be no time. It takes months to learn the game properly.'

'Oh, but I shall be here for months. You were back awfully late—or perhaps you were wandering round the house looking for something—or *someone*.'

'Of course I wasn't,' Lamia exclaimed, firing up. 'You have no——'

But Catriona interrupted quickly, 'Do you take your shower every morning or every afternoon?'

Her mind still on the previous question, Lamia said unthinkingly, 'In the afternoon, of course. But I——' She broke off as she saw Catriona start to grin.

Turning to Lucas, Catriona said, 'Thank you so much for finding that cream to put on my mosquito bites last night. I did look for a first-aid kit but I couldn't find one. Don't we have one?'

'Of course,' Lucas replied. He looked across at the other woman. 'Lamia keeps it locked away. Don't you, Lamia? Probably in the same place that you keep the mosquito nets. Why didn't you put one in Catriona's room?'

Her face flushing, Lamia shrugged. 'She only had to ask for one.'

'No, Lamia, you should have provided it, as you know full well.' His voice curt now, Lucas stood up. 'Mohamed, I want to talk to you.'

The two men went out of the room and across the hall to the finds room, shutting the door behind them. Lamia, her face flushed, sat on for only a couple of minutes, then she got abruptly to her feet and followed them.

Bryan chuckled. 'Good for you, girl; I was sure she'd been using more than her fair share of water. Lucas taxed the servants about it, but Lamia hires and fires them and they're all afraid of her, so he could never prove it.'

'Till now,' Mike added. Looking at Catriona, he apologised for his unspoken condemnation. 'Sorry.'

'That's OK. Lucas said he'd arranged for me to go to the French dig this morning. Is the site far?'

'A couple of miles. They're excavating one of the temples.'

'Do you think Lucas will lend me the Land Rover?'

'Better ask him,' Bryan said, looking up as Lucas came back into the room.

'Ask me what?'

'Catriona wants to know if she can borrow the car to go over to the French site.'

He shook his head. 'I'd better take you. Then I can introduce you to their expert.'

'When do you want to leave?'

'As soon as you're ready.'

'I'm ready now.' She pushed her plate away, stood up, and picked up her bag, which she swung on her shoulder.

'Such enthusiasm,' Lucas said, but more in amusement than mockery. He moved towards the door, but then turned. 'By the way, in future there will be enough water for each of us to have an extra shower per week.'

The two men cheered and Catriona was laughing to herself as they came out of the house. Lucas, looking at her face, immediately guessed why.

'Now you don't have to go without a shower next week.'

'That's right.' Catriona longed to ask him what he'd said to Mohamed and Lamia but decided it would be prudent not to.

'You handled that situation OK,' he told her. 'And I don't mean the shower issue.'

'You could have handled it just as easily. More easily, probably.'

He nodded, but said, 'When two women start arguing it's better to keep out of the way.'

She wrinkled her nose at him, which made him laugh. Walking towards the Land Rover, he said, 'I think you'll be able to learn a lot from——' He broke off as another car came through the gate into the compound. A big black Mercedes that Catriona had no difficulty in recognising. It pulled up beside them and the chauffeur hurried to open the door for Omar Rafiq to get out.

CHAPTER FOUR

CATRIONA gave a small gasp, making Lucas's eyes narrow as he looked at them both. Omar smiled at them, a smile that took it for granted that he would be made welcome no matter on what terms they had all parted.

'Ah, Dr Kane. How good to see you again. A lovely morning.'

'And an extremely early one, for you,' Lucas returned, dispensing with the niceties. 'What brings you here, Omar?'

But Omar turned to Catriona, took her hand, and bowed over it. 'My dear Miss Fenton—Catriona. How very pleasant to see you again.'

'Good morning,' Catriona returned. 'How are you and your daughters?'

'I am well, thank you. But my poor little girls...' Omar spread his hands expressively.

'Why, what's the matter with them?'

But he wouldn't say, just shook his head dismally.

'You haven't yet told me what you want,' Lucas pointed out, breaking brutally in on his apparent sadness.

'I wish to talk to you.'

'You could have done that over the phone.'

'But this is a matter of some—delicacy.'

'You'll have to wait, then; I'm taking Miss Fenton to another site. I'll talk to you when I get back, in about an hour.' And Lucas put his hand on her arm to propel her towards the Land Rover.

'But what I want to say concerns Catriona, so perhaps it would be better if she stayed.'

They both turned to look at Omar. 'Do you know anything about this?' Lucas asked her, his voice hardening.

'No, of course not.'

'Just what do you want, Omar?'

'Perhaps we could talk in private,' Omar suggested. 'The car is air-conditioned.'

Lucas rejected that out of hand. Glancing at Omar's beautifully cut suit and shiny shoes, he said, 'All right, if you want to talk in private; let's take a drive up to the dig.' And he pulled open the door of the old Land Rover, standing dusty and pitted beside the gleaming limousine.

Omar shrugged and got in beside them as they drove through the gate and out across the morning-clean sand to the excavation site. As soon as they reached it and got out Catriona realised why Lucas had chosen to come out here to the desert. For all he was an Egyptian and this was his country, Omar looked out of place here; he belonged to the city and business. But Lucas, in his stone-coloured shorts and shirt, his light hair and tanned skin, was in his element, at one with the desert as he learned its hidden secrets.

They walked round the site for a while, then Lucas turned to Omar. 'Well?'

'I'm glad we've come here,' Omar said, gesturing towards the dig. 'It was about your excavation that I wished to speak to you.'

'You said it was about Catriona.'

'It is about both.'

Lucas gave a short laugh. 'Now I know why you wanted her here.'

'Why?' Catriona asked.

Both men ignored her.

'I want nothing more to do with you, Omar,' Lucas said shortly.

'Maybe you don't,' Catriona put in, 'but I want to know how I come into this?'

'Perhaps I could talk to you alone for a moment,' Omar said to Catriona quickly, before Lucas could speak.

The latter laughed again but didn't try to stop him, just shrugged and walked away.

When he was out of earshot, Omar said pleadingly, 'It is my children, my little girls. Unfortunately I could not find another tutor for them.' He smiled. 'But that is not what is the matter; they were very pleased I could not find anyone. You see, they both liked you so much that they don't want anyone else. I am sure it is because you are young and you swam and played with them. Most of their teachers at school are much older, I think.'

'Mr Rafiq, I've——'

'Omar,' he corrected.

She shrugged, thinking that he seemed different today from the man who had held her in his house against her will, far more conciliatory. 'All right, Omar. I've already said that I can't——'

He held up his hand. 'Yes, I know. But Nadia and Dorreya have been begging me to ask you again. I am away so much, you understand, and they are lonely with only Mrs Aziz for company.'

'But surely you could find someone younger to be with them?'

Shrugging his shoulders, Omar said, 'I had counted on the woman from England. All the other suitable companions have already got posts for the summer. And, besides, I want them to learn some English before they start the subject at school. And I am sure you are the right person to teach them; in just one day they learned from you. You will be a very good tutor for them.'

'That's kind of you to say so, but you know that I'm committed to this job,' she answered stiffly.

'Yes, I understand that, and respect you for it,' he added flatteringly. 'But I have thought of a way that you could do both. A way for you to divide your time between here and the Garden of the Nile.'

She frowned. 'I don't want to divide my time.'

'But you will not be so hard as not to listen to my idea, surely?'

'All right. How?' she asked with a shrug.

'Dr Kane needs money so that he can go on with his excavations. Did you know that?' And when she shook her head, he went on, 'I am willing to make a donation towards his running costs—is that the right expression?—in return for allowing you to come and teach my children for three days a week. And I will of course pay you half the wages I promised you.'

'That seems an awful lot of money just to get me to teach your daughters,' Catriona said warily.

'Yes, I know,' Omar surprised her by saying. 'But I intended to sponsor Dr Kane's excavation team before. However, something occurred and we had a disagreement. I was sorry that it happened and have been looking for some way of giving him this money, and this seems to be a good excuse that will not offend him.'

'He hasn't said anything about being short of money.'

'He is hardly likely to talk about his financial difficulties to you.'

Suppressing her anger at such a chauvinistic remark, Catriona said shortly, 'I doubt if he'll take it.'

'He will if he wants to continue his work through the summer. Shall I ask him?'

'I haven't yet said that I'm willing to accept your offer,' Catriona prevaricated, wondering just how badly Lucas needed money. He hadn't said that the dig was in danger of closing, but then, Omar had been right, he was hardly likely to take her, newly arrived from England, into his confidence.

'You haven't said no,' Omar pointed out. He smiled charmingly. 'And having experienced the conditions of the excavation house for a few days maybe the thought of spending three days a week at my house is more attractive to you. There is the pool and the bathrooms, the air-conditioning, the garden and——'

'Enough! Enough!' Catriona said, unable to prevent herself laughing at such an extraordinary form of bribery, and lifting a hand to stop him. She gave Omar a contemplative look. 'You were waiting until I'd found out how terrible the site house was before you came, weren't you?' she said in sudden intuition.

'Yes.' He inclined his head in agreement.

She didn't for a minute think that Lucas would agree to this, but just in case, she looked him straight in the eyes and said, 'I would have to have some personal guarantees from you before I'd even think of accepting your offer.'

'They are?'

'That you'd keep away from me,' she said bluntly. 'To me you would be no more than the girls' father. If you ever tried to go beyond that I would leave immediately, and there is no way you would keep me there against my will. Do you understand?'

He nodded. 'I promise that you will have no reason to complain. I would not have kept you before. It was to—tease Dr Kane, that's all.'

'And is this offer you're making me just to tease Dr Kane, too?'

With a laugh, Omar said, 'No, it is to stop my daughters making my life impossible with their pleas. I like a quiet life at home. So, will you accept?'

'I'm afraid it's immaterial; Lucas will never allow me to accept.'

'We shall see. Let's go and ask him.' They walked back to where Lucas stood, leaning against one of the ruined walls, eyes narrowed as he watched them, and Omar said, 'I have heard that you are again short of money to keep your team working.'

'The British Academy sponsors us,' Lucas returned brusquely.

'During the winter, yes, but not during the summer and autumn. It is only your own——' he searched for the word and found a tactful one '—your own en- thusiasm that keeps you here now.'

'So?' Lucas neither confirmed nor denied it.

'So you are looking for sponsors once again.' He paused and Catriona saw Lucas tense. 'If you re- member, I once before offered to sponsor your excavation.'

'And I remember how you went back on your word— *and why*.' Lucas shot the last two words at him like bullets from a gun.

Omar shrugged and opened his hand expressively. 'Really, Dr Kane, all that is behind us now. I am sur- prised you even bother to refer to that little— misunderstanding.'

'*I* understood it perfectly,' Lucas told him, his face grim.

'But I wish to take an interest in your work and to sponsor you to this——' Omar took a cheque from his pocket and handed it to Lucas '—amount. Now. Today. The money is yours.'

Lucas read the cheque, his eyes widening incredu- lously. Then he gave a short laugh. 'I'll say this for you, Omar, when you decide to bribe someone you do it in a big way.'

Not at all offended, Omar nodded. 'It is enough to keep your site working until September, is it not?'

'You've nicely calculated it to do just that,' Lucas agreed. 'And do I need to ask what you want in return?'

'Possibly not. I require Catriona's—services.'

'Do you, by God? And has she agreed to your request?'

'Hey!' Catriona cut in. 'You can ask me, you know. I am here.'

But the two men were looking each other in the eyes, Lucas's face contemptuous, Omar's taunting.

'Oh, yes, I think so. But I would not deprive you of her entirely. I have suggested that she works for you for three days of the week and spends three more at my house. On the seventh day, she will, of course, need to rest.'

'So it would seem,' Lucas said on a note of heavy sarcasm. 'And do you really think I'll agree to that?'

'Catriona has—so why shouldn't you?' Lucas's head came up sharply at that and he swung to look at her. But before either of them could speak Omar added smoothly, 'That's if you want to keep on with the excavation, of course.' And he nodded at the cheque that Lucas still held in his hand.

Lucas's lips thinned as he continued to look at Catriona. 'How much is he offering you?' he said sardonically.

'A bath and a swim in his pool,' she replied flippantly.

He blinked, and for a moment his eyes searched her face, then he put a hand on her arm and drew her to one side. 'Have you forgotten how he tried to hold you against your will before? How can you even contemplate going with him?'

Annoyed that he was putting the onus on her, she said shortly, 'He told me he only did that to make you angry. And after the way I've seen you standing up to each other, I'm not surprised. Are you sure there's only money between you two?'

Ignoring the question, Lucas said tersely, 'Have you given even a minute's real thought to what you're letting yourself in for? Arab men go for European women because they're different, but they have no respect for women they can buy.'

'Now just a minute! Just what the hell do you think he's offering me?'

A guarded look came into Lucas's eyes. 'Suppose you tell me.'

'He wants me to tutor his children during the summer holidays. And that's *all*.'

'And you believe that?'

'Yes! Because that's what he mistook me for in the first place.'

'You don't really think that's all he wants, do you?'

'It's all he's going to get,' she answered bluntly, growing ever more angry that Lucas could suspect her of being willing to accept anything else. 'And I've made him promise he won't try anything.'

'You can't trust him, Catriona,' Lucas said urgently. 'Believe me. I know.'

'Very likely. But I can take care of myself,' she told him, the anger making her stubborn.

Lucas laughed aloud in disbelief at that. 'I wonder how many millions of girls have said that and lived to regret it.'

'And if he does try anything,' Catriona went on as if she hadn't heard, 'I can always threaten him that you'd sort him out. I rather think you'd like that, wouldn't you?'

He gave a ghost of a grin. 'Perhaps—but I'd rather not have reason to.'

'You won't have. But I don't have to accept his offer. If you tell me not to, then I won't.'

He gave her a rather strange look. 'Is that what you want—for me to order you not to?'

Catriona frowned, not understanding him. 'Omar said you needed the sponsorship money. That you haven't enough to keep going until next winter.'

Lucas's eyes drew into a frown. 'You're not accepting for that reason, are you?' She didn't answer at once, and he said sharply, 'Do you want to accept Omar's offer or don't you?'

Catriona didn't, but she remembered how she'd been out of work, back in England. If tutoring Omar's children meant that Lucas would be able to keep the dig open and keep her on here until next year, then she'd willingly take on the extra job. *It wasn't what I came out here to do, but it will only be till his children go back to school. I can stand it for that long,* she told herself. She raised hazel eyes to meet his and merely shrugged, letting him make the decision, knowing how torn he must be.

Lucas had seen her hesitate and his lips thinned into a sardonic line. 'Could you fight Omar off for that long? He'll want value for his money, you know.'

Catriona smiled a little. 'I've been fighting men off for several years now; I think I've become an expert.'

'*Always* fighting them off?' he asked quizzically, momentarily diverted.

'Yes.'

He didn't look as if he believed her but came to a decision. Turning, Lucas walked back to Omar. To her inner consternation, because she'd been sure he'd refuse, she heard him say, 'I've decided to let Catriona accept your offer, Omar.'

Omar didn't much like the way Lucas put it, but he merely smiled and said, 'I'm very glad.'

'She can start working for you on Monday—and then work every Saturday, Monday and Wednesday.'

'I would prefer that she works on consecutive days,' Omar objected.

'Sorry. You said three days and those are the only ones on which I'm willing to let her go.'

As much as she hated to be spoken of like this, to be treated as if she wasn't there, Catriona stayed quiet, letting the two men sort this out between them.

'And I'll also come and meet her and bring her back here every night,' Lucas added, his eyes daring Omar to argue.

'How solicitous you're being over Catriona's welfare,' the Arab mocked. 'And so unnecessarily. She and I have a complete understanding in this matter. I have already assured her that she will be quite safe under my roof. Can you give her the same assurances when she is under *your* roof, my dear Dr Kane?'

Lucas's face hardened. 'Those are my terms, Omar. Take them or leave them.'

'I will take them, of course,' Omar said smoothly. 'It will be inconvenient, but that's all. But tomorrow is Saturday—why can't she start then?'

'Because from past experience of dealing with you, I'm going to make sure the cheque is cleared first. Don't you think that's wise?'

It was meant to be insulting, and could quite easily have pushed Omar into taking offence and changing his mind. Perhaps it was meant to. Omar's eyes narrowed dangerously, but then he gave a slow smile and merely said, 'Very wise. Shall we shake hands on the—er—deal?'

'Of course,' Catriona interrupted, inwardly fuming but determined not to let it show. She held out her own hand. 'Will you send your car for me on Monday? What time?'

'Shall we say eight o'clock?' Omar said in some amusement as he shook her hand.

'Eight will be fine. We'll take you back to the house.' And Catriona walked over to the Land Rover, putting an end to any further baiting.

They dropped Omar off at the house, and Lucas immediately drove off again towards the French site.

'We're late,' he muttered, putting his foot down and sending up a great cloud of dust behind them.

Catriona sat beside him, still hardly able to believe that Lucas had allowed her to go and work for Omar. She'd been sure that he'd not only resist but tell Omar to get lost. He must need the sponsorship money really badly. But then she remembered that there had been other implications and said bluntly, 'Why did Omar change his mind about sponsoring you before?'

'It doesn't concern you,' Lucas replied, equally blunt.

'If I'm in the middle of you, then I think it does,' she objected.

'He just went back on his word,' Lucas said shortly.

'Did you give him reason to?'

An amused glint came into his eyes. 'Possibly.'

'Is that all there is between you—just money?'

'Isn't it enough? Look, drop it, will you, Catriona? The reasons are—personal and private.'

His tone was curt and she knew she wouldn't get anything else out of him. She sat back in her seat, wondering if it really was only money. Where did the girl, Elaine, who'd once slept in her room, come into all this? Maybe she didn't. Maybe only Lucas had been involved with her. But it all seemed so strange. Surely Lucas wouldn't have antagonised a man who was going to sponsor the dig for no good reason? Glancing across at his hard, lean profile, Catriona realised how little she had learned about him. Only that he was determined and ambitious, obsessed with his work. To the exclusion of all else? That she wasn't sure about, although taking Omar's sponsorship would seem to point that way. But she knew that beneath his outer shell of hardness there was kindness. Why else would he have stayed to anoint the bites she couldn't reach? A really hard man would just have thrown the salve at her and told her to get on with it—if he'd bothered to find it for her at all.

'What are you thinking?' Lucas demanded, breaking into her reverie.

'What do you think I'm thinking?' she countered.

They reached the other site, Lucas pulled the car up with a jerk and raised his eyes to heaven. 'Women!'

The French textile expert was a dapper little man who managed to look smart even here in the desert. Lucas introduced them and abandoned her as he went off to drink a glass of wine with the French field director before driving away again. Catriona learned a lot that day, but she also learned that she needn't sell herself short. After a kind of oral test, the Frenchman complimented her on all the reading she'd done and told her that all she needed was some hands-on experience with ancient pieces of cloth, which he proceeded to give her.

It was a fascinating day, and they both enjoyed themselves, the Frenchman happy to share his skill and show off his expertise, and Catriona grateful to learn and full of awe at the age of the pieces she was handling. A tunic over three thousand years old that had been carefully darned and darned over again because cloth was so precious. A sleeveless shirt that still had the crease marks from where it had been folded to put in the owner's tomb when he'd died around 2000 BC. She looked and examined with reverence.

At four o'clock the field director came into the room they were working in and invited Catriona to stay to dinner. It seemed that on Fridays the French team gave their cook the day off and prepared the food themselves. It was delicious, the best food Catriona had tasted since she came to Egypt. The team were friendly too; bigger than the English team, it had two women, one of them the director's wife, and the whole atmosphere seemed more relaxed and sociable. Luckily Catriona spoke French quite well so that she was drawn easily into the conversation.

Lucas came to collect her and drove her, feeling comfortably full and drowsy, back to their own house. When they reached it they found that they were the only ones there, all the others having gone into Luxor in Mohamed's car. Lucas took a couple of cans of beer from the fridge and handed one to her, obviously expecting her to drink it out of the can. After watching her struggle with the stiff ring pull for a few moments, he took the can from her, opened it with a sharp fizz of air, then went into the kitchen and came back with a glass.

'Here.' He handed it to her. 'You don't look as if you know your way round a can.'

Catriona did, but she wasn't about to spoil his gesture. 'Thanks.'

He sat down in the armchair opposite hers. There was no fireplace in the room, but the map on the wall provided a focal point. 'How did you get on today?'

'Very well. The French textile man was like a living museum; he knows so much about Egyptian cloth and artefacts.'

'Yes, he's the best around. I hope you thanked him for giving you his time.'

'Of course. And thank *you* for arranging it for me.'

Lucas shrugged it off and took a swig of his beer. 'When we were talking the other day you said that you'd been out of work before you came here. For how long?'

'About three months.'

'How did you live?'

'The same way as all the other hundreds of thousands of people who're out of work—on the dole.'

'Where were you living?'

'In London. When I was working I had my own bedsit, and I managed to keep that on for a while, but I couldn't get the money they owed me out of the company I worked for, so I had to give it up and go and stay with a friend.'

'A man-friend?' Lucas asked, his eyes on her face.

She didn't look away but met his gaze quite openly. 'No, it was a girl, an old friend from college—but why do you ask?'

'Perhaps to find out if you really do have enough experience to hold off Omar.'

Catriona smiled a little. 'Haven't you got it the wrong way round; I don't need experience of men, only in keeping them at a safe distance?'

'And you think you have that?'

'Oh, definitely,' she said with assurance.

Lucas let his eyes run over her. 'I can't believe that a girl with your looks and figure is completely inexperienced.'

'You may believe or not believe whatever you like,' she returned calmly, in no way put out.

'You didn't exactly fight me off when I came to your room the other night,' Lucas pointed out.

'I took it that, as the leader of this team, you're also responsible for our health and well-being. So I accepted your help as if you were a doctor or nurse or something. And I was truly grateful.'

That made him laugh, his eyes crinkling, and she thought how attractive he looked when he did so. There was something hard, perhaps even a little harsh in his face when in repose, but his laugh transformed him.

'*Do* you have any first-aid training?' she asked him.

'None whatsoever,' Lucas admitted. 'But don't get too worried; we have a comprehensive first-aid kit and a phone. I've enough common sense to deal with minor injuries with the former, and to pick up the latter and call an ambulance if anything worse happens.'

'And has anything bad ever happened?'

'One of the workmen managed to cut himself quite badly once, but apart from that our most common ailment seems to be Egyptian tummy.'

'Ugh! I hope I don't get it,' Catriona said, making a face.

'You will. Everybody does, even hardened Egyptologists.'

'Like you?'

'Like me,' he admitted.

'So who looks after you when you're unwell?' she asked lightly. 'Lamia?'

Lucas's lips twitched. 'Usually I'm abandoned to my fate. Lamia is much too busy visiting her friends in Luxor to act as a nurse.'

'She doesn't seem to look after this house very well,' Catriona said bluntly. 'The French house is much better than this.'

'Yes, I know, but it's the custom for the wife of one of the team members to act as housekeeper. It means they can be with their husband and you don't have to pay them too much. So Lamia does the job, however reluctantly. Anyway, there isn't anyone else.'

'Aren't Mike or Bryan married?'

He shook his head. 'No. Bryan was but his wife left him—couldn't stand coming to Egypt all the time.'

'And you?' she asked casually, then answered it for him, 'No, of course you're not.'

His left eyebrow rose quizzically. 'Why so certain?'

'If you were married you'd make sure your wife was out here doing Lamia's job.'

He grinned. 'Perhaps.'

Encouraged by his smile, she went on, 'I can just picture the woman you'd choose.'

Lucas settled back in his chair, an amused look in his eyes. 'Describe her.'

'All right.' She put her head to one side, considering him. 'I think she'd be very capable, very efficient, not at all feminine or fussy. Probably not an Egyptologist, more likely an ex-secretary who can type up all your records and manuscripts. A good cook who wouldn't get flustered if you brought home half a dozen guests to take pot luck,' she added, warming to her theme.

The amused look in Lucas's face had deepened. 'And what would she look like, this paragon?'

Catriona frowned. 'That's more difficult.' Then her face cleared. 'I know! She would be one of two types: either the "county" type, who in England would wear a cardigan and pearls, and have neat, short hair; or else a sixties flower-child type who wears long skirts and loose, embroidered blouses and open sandals, and has long straight hair, and probably wears a wide-brimmed straw hat,' she finished triumphantly.

'Good grief!' Lucas gave her a pained look. 'Do you really think those are the kind of women that turn me on?'

She gave him a surprised look. 'You want a wife who's *sexy* as well as all these other qualities? Sorry, Lucas, but you don't stand a chance.'

He burst out laughing, the deep, masculine sound of it filling the room. 'I haven't had too much difficulty before.'

'The vanity of the man! But we're talking wives here, not casual affairs.'

'So you don't think I'd have any luck winning a sexually attractive woman for a wife?'

'Afraid not. Not with your lifestyle.'

'Then it looks as if I'm going to have to stay a bachelor, because the thought of either of the two types you described absolutely terrifies me!' They both laughed, then he said, 'And how about you? Shall I describe the kind of man I think you would go for?'

'You can't. He doesn't exist,' she said lightly, finding herself strangely reluctant to hear him make guesses about the subject.

'Coward! You did it to me.'

'It was only in fun.'

'Was it? And are you afraid that you wouldn't find it fun if I did it to you?' He was looking at her closely now, his eyes intent on her face.

Flushing a little, Catriona said rather defiantly, 'OK, go ahead.'

'All right. Now let's see...' Pyramiding his hands, he rested his chin on them. 'You say you haven't much experience of men, which is a rare thing in a girl nowadays. But then, all things are relative; what you call little might have been thought of as a lot twenty years ago.' She flashed him a 'watch-it' look and he grinned. 'But I think the man you choose would have to be very special, to be quite a man to deserve you.'

She was pleased but tried not to show it. 'What would he be like?' she asked, interested now.

'Don't you know?'

'What do you mean?'

'Haven't you already met the man you want?'

'I told you; he doesn't exist.'

'Not even in your imagination, in your dreams?'

Catriona shook her head. 'Dreams are no use to anyone. They just stop you facing reality.'

Frowning a little, Lucas said, 'That's a very cryptic remark. Don't tell me you've been disappointed in love?'

'I don't intend to. You were about to describe the man you think will suit me,' she reminded him.

He gave her a speculative glance but nodded and looked pensive. 'Well, now, he'd obviously have to be tall and——'

He broke off as a car pulled up outside and then came the sound of several pairs of feet entering the house, and

the rest of the team walked into the room. Lucas glanced
at her and said softly, 'Now you'll just have to imagine
him for yourself.'

Everyone was in a brighter mood tonight, after their
trip to Luxor. Bryan and Mike had been to an ex-pats
club they belonged to where they had swum, played
billiards, and had a traditional English lunch of roast
beef and Yorkshire pudding. It seemed to have done them
good; they both looked relaxed and were quite talkative.
Even Lamia and Mohamed chatted for ten minutes
before Mohamed put the television set on.

The next couple of days were uneventful, following
the usual working pattern, except that Lucas went into
Luxor first thing on Saturday morning, and on the
Sunday told Catriona that Omar's cheque had been
cleared. So now there was no going back. Catriona didn't
sleep very well at night; apart from the terrible bed she
couldn't help but wonder what she was letting herself in
for, and whether she really could keep Omar at arm's
reach if she had to. She was used to Western men who,
however randy they might feel, still lived by a certain
set of rules. Arab men might have very different ones.

So she was feeling tired and trying to hide any un-
certainty beneath a bright exterior on the Monday
morning. Lamia was still in bed and the others had all
gone to the dig when she came down into the hall to
wait for the car. With Mrs Aziz and Arab custom in
mind, she had put on a denim skirt and a long-sleeved
T-shirt, and carefully plaited her hair. There was the
sound of an engine entering the courtyard so she went
outside, but it was the Land Rover.

Lucas got out and his mouth thinned a little as his
eyes went over her clothes. They settled on her face, saw
the dark smudges of tiredness, and grew grim. 'You don't
have to do this, you know. It isn't too late to change
your mind.'

'Why should I want to do that?' Catriona countered, suddenly longing for him to tell her not to go.

But he only said, 'Maybe it was bravado before. Now that the time has actually come, you may have realised just what you're letting yourself in for.'

Disappointed, she shook her head. 'I'm fine. Don't worry about me.'

'Is that what I'm doing?' He gave a short laugh. 'You must arouse my paternal instincts.'

'*Really*?'

Catriona sounded so shocked that Lucas laughed. 'I think it would be better if I didn't answer that.' Then his face grew stern again. 'Seriously, Catriona, if you've changed your mind, now is the time to say.'

'But then you'd have to give the money back and wouldn't be able to go on with the dig.'

'Forget the dig,' he said shortly. 'Don't do this if you have the least misgivings.'

Resolutely she shook her head and gave him a bright smile. 'I haven't. I'll be fine.'

He studied her face intently for a moment, then his own features seemed to set, become masklike. 'Very well,' he said coolly. 'You're obviously quite happy with the set-up.' He glanced at his watch. 'Omar's car should be here any minute.'

Catriona expected him to go but he stayed the few moments it took for the Mercedes to enter the courtyard, exactly on time. It drew up in front of them and the chauffeur got out. Lucas asked him a crisp question in Egyptian and the driver replied. Lucas nodded, apparently in satisfaction, then he bade her a brief goodbye. 'I'll be over at seven tonight to pick you up.'

'OK. Thanks.' She got into the car and glanced back through the rear window to see him standing in the doorway watching her go, his fists on his hips. Catriona half lifted her hand to wave to him, but then thought better of it; somehow that was suddenly too friendly a gesture. In just a few minutes he had become cool and aloof towards her again, although she couldn't think why.

CHAPTER FIVE

OMAR wasn't at the house, he was in Cairo. It was the first thing Mrs Aziz told Catriona when she got to the Garden of the Nile. And whatever Omar's real reason for employing her, he'd spoken the truth about the girls; they were delighted to see her, running excitedly across the courtyard to meet her and eagerly trying to make themselves understood, failing, but smiling widely to show that they were pleased.

They spent the morning looking through the children's toys, with Catriona writing the English words for them in large letters on pieces of paper and sticking them to the dolls and books and games. Lunch was delicious, almost as good as that cooked by the French team, and a whole lot better than they got at the excavation house. While the girls rested after it, Catriona relaxed and sunbathed on a lounger by the pool, letting her thoughts wander. It had been rather an anti-climax finding that Omar wasn't here; she'd been preparing herself to rebuff him and now there was no need. There was still no Mrs Rafiq around. Catriona could have asked the girls about their mother, she supposed, but the language was a barrier and also she didn't want to upset them in any way if their parents were separated or divorced. And Mrs Aziz was totally uncommunicative.

Whatever Omar was like in his personal life, he must certainly be wealthy, she thought as she slid into the water and began to swim lazily up and down. Egypt was a poor country and anyone who could afford this house and another one in Cairo must be seriously rich. Now that she'd seen a little more of the country she realised just how successful he must be.

Catriona turned to do another length and her thoughts switched to Lucas. He, too, was successful in his own field, although it would probably never be a spectacularly lucrative one. But where a politician gained power and an entrepreneur money, an archaeologist could gain prestige, which would be with him all his life. His work, though often slow and painstaking, would fascinate him always, and probably give him far more satisfaction out of life than any whiz-kid got from making money. It would be a quieter, narrower life, in which the thrill of discovering a new tomb would be far, far greater than making a killing on the stock-market.

That thought, in regard to Lucas, suddenly made Catriona laugh and swallow water, so that she had to stop swimming. Lucas? Leading a quiet life? Somehow she just couldn't see it. He had far too much restless energy and ambition. He, too, was going places, and Egyptology was merely a step in that direction.

There were lessons again in the afternoon, she had dinner with the girls, then Lucas arrived to collect her.

'You don't look as if you put up much of a fight,' he commented, his eyes going over her as she got into the car.

'I didn't have to,' Catriona answered with a grin. 'Omar wasn't there.'

He didn't look at all surprised and she guessed that he'd already found that out from the chauffeur. 'How did you get on?'

'Fine. The girls were pleased to see me, and I enjoyed teaching them.'

'More than you enjoy your work at the dig?'

'No, of course not. That's part of my career.'

'Your career is important to you, isn't it?' Lucas said on a reflective note.

'Yes, very much so. I worked hard for my degree, and I'm not about to let all that work go to waste.'

'Not even for marriage and a family?' he asked, in an overly casual tone.

She turned her head to look at him, his face all angles and shadows in the light of the setting sun that shone through the windscreen. 'It's possible to have both, I suppose,' she said cautiously, wondering where he was heading.

'You don't sound very sure.'

'No, I'm not—and nor are you.'

'Why me?'

'Well, you're not married either, and you're much older than me.'

'As old as an Egyptian mummy,' he agreed facetiously, and pulled a woebegone face.

Catriona laughed, and suddenly felt happy. 'But I'm not completely against marriage,' she felt compelled to add.

To her gratified surprise, Lucas said, 'Well, that's good.' Then spoilt it all by adding, 'I must remember to tell Omar that.'

'Omar? Why him?'

'Didn't you know? His wife died a couple of years ago and he's on the lookout for a new bride.'

'Really?' At first Catriona was so taken aback that she could think of nothing else to say, but then, her voice hardening, said, 'Is that why you asked my views on marriage?'

'Of course. He'll be more circumspect when I tell him.'

'I don't understand. Why should it make Omar act any differently?'

'Because to Omar there are two types of women: those who are his equals in birth and wealth, and those who are not. The first are eligible marriage partners, the rest are to take to bed if they're attractive or striking enough—and available.'

'What are you trying to tell me, Lucas?' Catriona said stiffly.

'That you definitely don't come into the first category. Omar will only ever marry a woman approved of by his family, one who will enhance his prestige and probably his wealth. The daughter of a noble or rich family. So don't get any ideas in that direction, Catriona.'

'I don't have any.'

'Not yet, perhaps. But going to his house regularly, sampling his wealth, you wouldn't be the first girl to be seduced by that kind of lifestyle.' He glanced across at her. 'But never forget that Omar sees you only in the second category, and he's attracted to you—he'll try to seduce you, if he can.'

'I think you're leaving one type of woman out of your classification,' Catriona said shortly. 'Those who are self-sufficient, and not interested in men just as a meal-ticket for life. And I've already proved that I'm not interested in money by not accepting his offer to work for him in the first place.'

'True,' Lucas admitted, then grinned. 'But you hadn't seen the excavation house then. And you weren't too reluctant to accept his offer the second time he asked.'

'That was to help you out,' she said in indignation.

'Are you kidding yourself that you're there for altruistic motives?' Lucas said jeeringly. 'No way. You're there for the same reason that Lamia is always sneaking in an extra shower; so that you can be clean and comfortable. You're like every other woman and crave good living and good food. You like luxury—and don't try to deny it,' he added as Catriona went to open her mouth in protest. 'You've been living poor, Catriona, and there's no way Omar's wealth isn't going to turn your head. Especially when he starts to try to seduce you by giving you presents.'

'He wasn't even there!' she exclaimed angrily.

'He will be.'

'Well, thanks for the warning,' she said through gritted teeth. 'But I'm not as naïve as you obviously think. I'm quite capable of working things out for myself, *and* of seeing through any pass Omar might make.'

Pulling up outside the site house, Lucas turned to look fully at her. 'Catriona,' he said pityingly, 'you're nothing but a babe in arms when compared to Omar. He was born knowing how to seduce women.'

She laughed, but there was no amusement in it. 'Well, if I get into difficulties all I have to do is to call out the cavalry: namely, Dr Lucas Kane. And then you'll have an excuse to sort Omar out—which I'm beginning to think is what you really want. What's the matter, Lucas?' she said tauntingly. 'Are you jealous of Omar and his wealth—or is it his success with women? Is that why you're so angry with him, because he knows how to get a woman and you don't?'

'If you were a man,' Lucas said grimly, 'I'd knock you from here to the other side of the yard.'

'But I'm not a man, am I?'

His eyes changed as he looked at her, darkened. 'No,' he said on a thickening note. 'But maybe you want me to prove to you that *I* am.'

He reached out for her. Catriona instinctively backed away. Fumbling for the door-handle, she quickly undid it, jumped out of the car, and hurried into the house, the sound of Lucas's amused laughter following her inside.

Coming back to the site house was a stark contrast to the Garden of the Nile. It was so cheerless; how Lucas could expect anyone, especially a woman, to enjoy living here, she couldn't imagine. But it could so easily be made more pleasant to live in, Catriona thought as she looked at her room as she washed and changed. Going down to the sitting-room, she felt the same would apply here. With the walls repainted, some new covers and cushions, curtains at the windows, and pictures instead of maps on the wall, it could look quite attractive.

Mike was in the room, looking over the top of his newspaper, watching her. 'You've got the look of a woman dissatisfied with her surroundings. Which probably means you want to redecorate or move the furniture.'

'I thought you didn't know much about women.'

'I know about my mother,' he said with feeling. 'She was forever moving the furniture around.'

Sitting down on the settee, Catriona said, 'Don't you think the place needs brightening up?'

His eyes went round the room, as if really looking at it for the first time. 'It looks all right to me. It's not fussy or cluttered with knick-knacks.'

'But it's dingy!'

'Well, yes, I suppose it must be a bit dull compared to Omar Rafiq's place,' Mike conceded.

'It's *more* than a bit dull compared to *any* other place. Surely you can see that the walls need repainting?'

'Yes, I see what you mean. They are rather scruffy.'

'Extremely scruffy. Good, I'm glad you agree. We'll get some paint and go over them.'

'I didn't say anything about painting the walls,' Mike said hastily. 'That's a job for the servants.'

'All right, we'll get the paint and set them to work. But we'll watch them to make sure they do it properly.'

'That's Lamia's job,' he protested.

'Which you know she won't do, or the place wouldn't be in this state.'

'Well, I don't see why I have to be involved,' Mike objected. 'It's nothing to do with me.'

Catriona rounded on him, her eyes wide in astonishment. 'You're not going to sit there and tell me that you're content to *wallow* in this filth, are you?'

'Yes,' he said valiantly, but quaking under her gaze.

'Rubbish! Of course you're not. We'll get Lucas to order the paint straight away.'

Mike immediately looked relieved. 'He won't do it.'

'Then I'll order it.'

'In that case you'll have to pay for it yourself, because you'll never get it out of Lucas. He'll never pay money out on anything that isn't vital to the dig.'

'But now that he's got Omar Rafiq to sponsor us he can surely spare enough money for a few tins of paint,' Catriona pointed out.

'Rafiq?' Mike queried. 'You're wrong there. He withdrew his sponsorship when he had that huge row with Lucas.'

'Yes, but now he's offered to sponsor him again. Didn't Lucas tell you?'

Mike shrugged. 'No. But we don't need his sponsorship; Lucas got a big oil company to finance us for the rest of the year.'

Catriona stared at him. 'Are you sure about that, Mike?'

'Of course. The directors of the company came to look round the dig and offered Lucas the money in front of Bryan.'

'Was this before Lucas rowed with Omar or after?'

'Oh, after. Only a couple of months ago. I don't suppose Lucas thought to mention it.'

'No, he didn't,' Catriona said shortly. 'But he's damn well going to tell me about it now.'

'I hardly think he'll want to discuss it.'

'Oh, won't he?' Catriona said determinedly. 'Just you wait and see.' She went in search of Lucas at once, full of fighting spirit, but it deflated when she found that he wasn't anywhere in the house. Come to think of it, she didn't remember him following her in after he'd brought her home; so maybe he'd gone straight out again. Going back to the sitting-room, she asked Mike if he'd seen him.

'He's gone to Cairo to give a lecture at the museum.'

'Tonight?' she asked in surprise.

'No, of course not. Tomorrow. Bryan drove him to the airport,' he added with some amusement.

Catriona gave him a look, but had to temporarily abandon her crusade and settle down to study for an hour or so before going to bed.

It seemed strange the next morning to have Bryan driving the jeep and issuing the orders. He did so competently enough, but he lacked Lucas's vitality, his ability to imbue everyone with his own enthusiasm, the hope that today might be the day when you unearthed something really interesting. Catriona expected Lucas to return that evening, but Bryan said he wasn't due back until the next day. The work went on as usual, and they spent the evening as they all normally did, working on finds, reading, or, in Mohamed's case, watching television, but somehow it wasn't the same. Catriona realised that Lucas was the spark that kept the team alive and eager, and she found she missed him.

She half expected that he wouldn't be back in time to collect her from Omar's house, but he was waiting in the car when she came out carrying a large bag which she tossed in the back. Forgetting how they'd parted, Catriona gave him a big smile and said, 'Hi. Did you have a good trip to Cairo?'

'Fine, thanks.'

'And your lecture; was it a success?'

'The audience seemed to enjoy it.'

'I wish I could have heard it,' she said with sincerity.

Lucas gave her a quick glance, as if he didn't quite believe her, but then said, 'I have the text; you can read it if you like.'

'Thanks, I'll read it tonight.'

He gave a small smile, then gestured with his head towards the back. 'What's in the bag?'

'That? Oh, it's a present.'

'From Omar? I told you he'd start giving you presents.'

It was Catriona's turn to smile. 'As a matter of fact it isn't from him; it's from Mrs Aziz.'

'And who is Mrs Aziz?'

'His housekeeper. The girls were asking me today about the dig. I drew them some pictures: of the site and the house, my room, and my bed. And I drew lumps of rock in the mattress and pillow to show how lumpy they were. Well, Mrs Aziz was watching, and just before I left she gave me a pillow to take home. Wasn't that kind of her? I didn't think she even liked me.'

'Maybe she just wants to make sure that you're comfortable where you are so there'll be less temptation to move into Omar's house,' Lucas said drily.

Annoyed, her pleasure in the gift spoilt, Catriona said, 'Must you cheapen every gesture? I'm sure she meant it kindly.'

He shrugged. 'Suit yourself.' He slowed to overtake a woman walking along with a sewing machine balanced on her head, narrowly missing one of the tattered and bleached shades that covered a street stall, then said, 'Is your bed really that bad?'

'It's terrible,' she said feelingly. 'Like trying to sleep on a stony beach.'

'*Trying* to sleep? Does it keep you awake, then?'

'Yes, of course. But it's much better with the mosquito net, and with this pillow it will be bliss.'

'Why didn't you tell Lamia about it?' Lucas asked on an exasperated note.

'I did. She said I'd just have to—to *lump* it.' And Catriona burst into laughter at her own pun.

Lucas laughed too, but afterwards said, 'So why didn't you tell *me* about it?'

'Because you don't strike me as the kind of man who wants to be bothered about anything as petty as the state of the new recruit's mattress and pillow,' she answered lightly. 'You're too obsessed with your work to care about things like that.'

'Is that how I strike you—as obsessed?'

'Yes.' But she added tactfully, 'Aren't most men obsessed by their work?'

'Possibly.' He abruptly changed the subject. 'Was Omar there?'

'No, I think he's away, in Japan.'

They drove on in silence, and had gone about a mile before Catriona said, 'Lucas, when do we get paid?'

'The first of the month. Short of money?'

'It's virtually non-existent.'

'How much do you want?'

'I don't know. I have no idea how much things cost here.'

Taking a hand off the wheel, he fished his wallet out of the back pocket of his jeans. 'Take a couple of hundred pounds out of here.'

'Two hundred—— Oh, Egyptian pounds, of course. That's just over thirty English pounds, isn't it?'

'About that.'

It wasn't a lot of money but she hoped it would be enough for what she wanted. 'Thanks.'

'It's a loan against your first month's salary,' he reminded her.

'Yes, of course.'

Catriona said nothing more, but after a few moments Lucas said, 'I know exactly what you're thinking; that if it hadn't been for you Omar wouldn't have given us the sponsorship money, and that the least I could do is *give* you those few pounds. Isn't that right?' She shook her head, but he went on, 'It doesn't work like that. You may be responsible for our continuing to work, but you don't get treated any differently from the others. As far as I'm concerned you're still just one of the team, same as everybody else.'

It was the opportunity Catriona had been looking for. Turning so that she could see his face, she said pointedly, 'But I'm not responsible for us continuing to work, am I?'

He shot her a glance. 'So you've found out we already have a sponsor.'

'Yes. So why take Rafiq's money?'

Lucas shrugged. 'There were reasons.'

'What reasons?'

'None that I'm prepared to discuss with you.'

She studied his face but could learn nothing from it. 'Was it because he let you down before and you wanted to teach him a lesson?'

'Could be.'

'What are you going to do with the money?'

'I expect I'll find a use for it,' he said unhelpfully.

And in the meantime I'm working for a man I both dislike and distrust, Catriona thought indignantly. Once more she felt like a pawn between the two men, but used by Lucas this time—and that hurt.

Lucas took his eyes off the road to look at her as she sat in silent thought. 'I hope you're not sulking about the money,' he said brusquely.

Her chin came up. 'Of course not,' she said curtly, and changed the subject by adding, 'And you were wrong, that wasn't what I was thinking at all.'

'No?'

'No.' She saw that he didn't believe her, so said, 'As a matter of fact I was wondering why Mrs Aziz always refers to Omar as Pasha Omar. Do you know what it means?'

'It's a title, the equivalent to lord or earl in English. Omar's family used to be among the Egyptian aristocracy. But titles like Pasha or Bey aren't supposed to be used in Egypt any more. He wouldn't be able to use it in public, but I suppose that his servants have always called the head of the family Pasha and it's become an unbreakable habit. Does it impress you?' he asked on a derisive note.

'No, of course not.'

But he didn't look as if he believed her.

And Catriona did look at Omar with new eyes when she went to the house on the following Saturday and found him there, back from his trip and taking a couple of days off work. For once he had discarded his dark business suit and was dressed casually, but it was still very smart, designer casual. She recognised that it would not do for Omar to wear old jeans and shirts to lounge around the house in; for him image was everything and therefore everything must be the best. He had brought presents back from Japan for the children and handed Catriona a small, gift-wrapped package. 'I have brought presents for everyone so you must have one also,' he told her.

Put like that it was difficult to refuse, but as she slowly opened the parcel the image of Lucas warning her about this very thing came sharply into Catriona's mind. Was this Omar's first step towards seducing her? she wondered. If so, she ought to refuse it, but she didn't particularly want to offend Omar if this was just an Arab tradition and there was nothing underhand in it at all. 'What did you bring the girls and Mrs Aziz?' she asked.

'Nadia and Dorreya had a miniature tea-set and Mrs Aziz a watch,' he told her. Adding, with amusement in his eyes, 'My chauffeur has a new pair of sunglasses, the cook a mixing machine, my secretary a radio... But do I need to go on?'

Catriona coloured and laughed. Reassured, she finished taking off the wrapping. He had bought her a silk evening bag, hand embroidered in the most delicate colours and beautifully designed and sewn. Her professional eye appreciated the workmanship as much as her feminine soul admired its beauty. 'Oh, how lovely!' she exclaimed. '*Thank you*. Look, Nadia, Dorreya, isn't it exquisite?'

They pulled her away to the playroom to look at their own present and the three of them spent an enjoyable hour pretending to be in England and having afternoon tea in the company of half a dozen dolls propped up round a small table.

Omar joined them for lunch and Catriona took the opportunity to make a request. 'I wonder if I might take the girls out sometimes?'

'Out?' Omar sounded surprised. 'Where would you wish to go?'

'Only into Luxor. I could take them round the shops so they could enlarge their vocabulary. And to the museum, and the temples. And perhaps to the *son et lumière*; they said they've never seen it. And I haven't either, so——'

'I could not possibly permit you to walk around Luxor unescorted,' Omar said shortly. He saw the look of disappointment that came into her eyes, although Catriona managed to quickly mask it, and added, 'But perhaps something could be arranged. I'll think about it.'

'Couldn't your chauffeur come with us?' she ventured. 'Or Mrs Aziz, if she has time?'

The housekeeper, hearing her name, obviously asked what she'd said. Omar told her and the woman shook her head vigorously.

'Mrs Aziz says that she has servants to do the shopping for her and does not wish to go with you. But the chauffeur is a good idea. I'll tell him to take you wherever you want to go.'

'Thank you.'

She nudged the girls and they said in unison and in English, 'Thank you, Daddy,' which made Omar laugh.

'I see you're training them well.'

'Can we go out this afternoon?' Catriona asked eagerly.

'So soon?'

'I need to buy some paint,' she explained.

'Some paint? Oh, you mean so that the girls can paint pictures?'

'Er—yes. Of course,' Catriona agreed, realising it might not be wise to tell Omar she wanted to go shopping for her own benefit as well.

'Very well, I'll tell the chauffeur to bring the car round after the girls have had their nap. Oh, and I would like to see you in my study in half an hour.'

Her senses wary, Catriona did as he asked and went to his room after lunch. But Omar was brisk and businesslike. 'I'm sorry I wasn't here last Monday to give you your first month's salary. Here it is.' And he handed her an envelope.

'In advance?'

'Certainly in advance.' Omar looked surprised. 'I pay all my staff that way.' He looked amused. 'I take it that Dr Kane does not?'

'We get paid on the first of the month,' Catriona explained.

He nodded, unlocked a drawer in his desk and took out a roll of notes, from which he peeled several off. 'You will also need some money for your expenses. To buy the paints and whatever else the girls need,' he enlarged, when Catriona looked at him in puzzled hesitation.

'Oh, I see.' Her face cleared. 'Yes. Thank you.'

'What do you usually do when the girls are sleeping?' he asked her.

'Sit by the pool,' she answered, wondering whether he thought she should be working, preparing lessons or something.

'Then let us do that.'

He walked out of the room without waiting for her to answer and she had little choice but to follow him. He pulled a couple of sun-loungers into the shade of a palm tree and gestured her towards one. Catriona sat on it but pulled the back up so that it was more like an elongated chair. Omar gave her an amused look. 'I think you are afraid of me, Catriona.'

'Do you? Do I have reason to be?'

He threw up his hands. 'You Westerners! You ask such direct questions. We Arabs prefer a little more subtlety.'

'Why—because it helps to avoid the issue?'

Omar laughed. 'You know, you are a refreshing change from Egyptian women.'

Realising that she wasn't going to get a straight answer out of him, Catriona said, 'Don't you know many Western women, then?'

'Oh, yes, I travel a great deal. And there are now more career women that one has to deal with,' he said on a disparaging note.

'Don't you like doing business with women?' Catriona asked innocently, keeping her amusement hidden.

But he glanced at her and smiled slightly. 'I suppose it depends on the woman. Some of them manage to keep their femininity but the others seem to think they have to become harder than men to be successful.'

'And which are the most successful?'

He shrugged. 'I avoid doing business with either type if I can.'

'Don't you have women working for you?'

'Egyptian women, yes; but as receptionists or in a clerical capacity.'

'You mean in subservient roles,' Catriona said shortly. 'Nothing that undermines the masculinity of the male staff members.'

'Ah, I see you are a feminist,' Omar remarked.

'No, but I believe in equality of opportunity.'

He was watching her face, especially her eyes as they sparked with fervour. 'But there can never be complete equality between men and women,' he said softly. 'Not when it is men who choose the woman they want, and men who keep women. And you must admit that women are kept, whether they be wives, daughters—or mistresses.'

Catriona couldn't believe it; how on earth had the conversation got round to that subject in such a short time? And when it was the one she most wanted to avoid, too! Standing up, she said briskly, 'If women had equal opportunities to work they wouldn't need to be kept. Think what a relief that would be for all you poor men. And now, if you'll excuse me, I'll go and make out a list of all the things I need to buy, before the girls wake up.'

Going up to the playroom, Catriona looked in the pay envelope Omar had given her; it was a cheque for exactly the amount they had agreed. Then she took the notes he'd given her for expenses out of her pocket and counted them. She stared, then went into a peal of laughter. He had given her three times as much to buy toys for his daughters than he had paid her for a whole month's work! Talk about Arabs being subtle; if she'd been rapacious for money that gesture would certainly have opened her eyes. As it was, it blew her argument about women becoming equal by work to shreds.

The chauffeur was a taciturn man who didn't say much, but he knew where the best shops were, and walked a couple of paces behind, keeping a watchful eye on them, so that they almost forgot he was there. They managed to find some paints and paper, several early reading books in English, and lots of other things that they all agreed were indispensable, which somehow managed to include some with-it clothes for the girls: shell-suits, loose trousers and shorts, and T-shirts with short sleeves in a whole range of bright colours.

The girls loved them, but Dorreya, round-eyed with excitement at their daring, said, 'My father...?'

'Don't worry,' Catriona assured her. 'He told me to buy what I liked.' Uncrossing her fingers, she consulted a phrase book she'd just bought. 'Now, I need to buy some paint. 'Dahaan,' she said to the chauffeur. 'Kahbeer aolbah,' and she used her hands to show him the size of tin she needed.

He looked amazed but shrugged and led them to the right shop. Catriona bought three large tins, which she hoped would be enough to do her room and the sitting-room. Then they went to another shop and she bought enough material to make curtains for the window in her room. It took all the money Lucas had given her but would, she was sure, be well worth it.

By this time they, and the chauffeur, were all loaded up with parcels. He wanted them all to go back to the car, but the female members of the party were having too good a time, so they went into a smart coffee-shop in a large store while the poor man staggered back to the car with all their shopping.

The Egyptians really knew how to make rich cakes. The girls filled her plate and made Catriona try them all. She ate *baklawa*, and a similar cake with layers of pastry stuffed with nuts and syrup, which Dorreya told her was called 'Eat and be thankful', and a type of doughnut, again with syrup, that was called 'Lady's Navel', a name that had the girls pealing with laughter.

The sound of their laughter caused two women who were passing to look round. Catriona glanced up and saw that one of them was Lamia. She nodded a greeting, expecting Lamia to walk by, but was amazed to hear Dorreya say, '*As-salaam alaykum*, Mrs Shalaby.'

Lamia stopped and came over, her cheeks a little flushed. She smiled at the girls and wished them good afternoon in return. Catriona understood that much, then lost it as they spoke to each other in Egyptian. Then Lamia looked at her. 'Hello, Catriona. I thought you were supposed to be teaching the children, not roaming about Luxor while their father is away.'

'Omar is back and was quite happy for us to come into town this afternoon. Are you here to order stores for the excavation house?' Catriona added pointedly.

Lamia gave her a glare, said a smiling goodbye to the girls, and walked away to rejoin her friend.

'You know Mrs Shalaby?' Catriona said to Dorreya.

'Yes. She—came to house.'

'Came? You mean she does not come now?'

Dorreya nodded, pleased to be understood. 'Yes. Not come long time.'

Interesting, Catriona thought. Had Lamia, then, been one of Omar's conquests? One of whom he'd now grown tired?

To find an answer to that question would be difficult, Catriona thought as they were driven back to the house. She definitely couldn't ask Lucas, or Omar, so who, then? Maybe Mike would know, but could he be persuaded to tell her? Probably not, at least not while Mohamed was still at the house, still a colleague. They reached the Garden of the Nile and she prudently stacked her own purchases out in the porch before going up-stairs with the girls to unpack all theirs.

It seemed that when Omar was home he worked in his study, where he wasn't to be disturbed, and then ate dinner late, about ten o'clock, but the women in the household ate much earlier, at six, so that the girls could go to bed at a reasonable hour. Catriona ate with them, said goodnight after the meal and let herself out to wait on the porch for Lucas to arrive. It always gave her pleasure to be out in the open for these few minutes. The fierce heat had died out of the day but the evening was still very warm. The Nile, such a short distance away, sent a gentle breeze to stir the trees in the garden, and the air was heavy with exotic, spicy scents. The musky perfume of the east. Leaning against one of the carved columns that supported the portico, Catriona closed her eyes and let the headiness wash over her.

A soft noise alerted her that someone was there. It was Omar. He was standing just a few inches away, his eyes fixed on her face. Instinctively she straightened, her back pressed against the stone.

'You're tired?' he asked, his voice soft, almost caressing.

'Oh, no. I was just enjoying the evening.'

But he ignored that and said, 'Dr Kane is working you too hard.'

'No harder than anyone else in the team—and anyway, I love the work.' Remembering, she fished in her pocket. 'I'm glad I've seen you. Here's what's left of the money you gave me for expenses. We spent rather a lot, I'm afraid.'

Omar smiled. 'So I understand. When the girls came in to say goodnight to me they told me all about it. They were still excited. You gave them a good day. It is what they need in their lives: a young woman to introduce them to a wider world.'

The unmistakable sound of the Land Rover's engine broke the stillness as the gates were opened for it and Lucas drove in.

Catriona was still holding the money out to Omar but instead of taking it he took some more money from his wallet and pushed it into her hand, timing it so that Lucas couldn't help but see as he drove up. 'You may take the girls out again and will need more money.' Then Omar put a hand on her arm and leaned to speak into her ear. 'Don't tell the girls, but I have planned a surprise for you all for next Saturday.'

That made her smile, as he'd intended it should; presenting a scenario that, to Lucas, looked as if they were sharing a pleasant and intimate secret.

Omar nodded to Lucas as he drew up, said goodnight to Catriona and went inside.

A very wise precaution, Catriona thought, as she saw the thundercloud look on Lucas's face. 'Hi.' She gave him a bright smile which he didn't return.

'Get in,' he ordered curtly.

'I have a couple of parcels to put in the back.'

He didn't offer to help her and she had to struggle with the box containing the tins of paint. When she got in beside him she was hot and feeling resentful.

'Don't tell me Mrs Aziz has given you another present?' Lucas said sarcastically.

'No, she hasn't.'

'So they're from Omar, are they?'

Guiltily remembering that Omar *had* given her a present, Catriona decided to attack. 'What the hell has it got to do with you if someone gives me a present?'

'So they are from him. I thought as much.'

'He brings everyone back a present when he goes away, even the cook and the gardener. It's a kind of Egyptian tradition.'

'He's the first Egyptian I've ever heard of who does it.'

'Well, maybe it's just a tradition in his family, then. How should I know? Anyway, what's it to you?'

'While you're working for me you're my responsibility. Why was he giving you money?'

Catriona sighed and opened her mouth to tell him, but then thought, Why the hell should I have to justify myself to him all the time? So instead she said shortly, 'I work for him. Why shouldn't he give me money?'

'It was your wages?'

'No.' She shot him a challenging look. 'Expenses.'

'That wad of notes he gave you was supposed to be for expenses!' Lucas gave a snort of derision. 'You little idiot! Can't you see that he's trying to buy you?'

'No, he isn't!'

'All right, to impress you with his wealth, then. And he's succeeding, too, by the look of it.'

Infuriated by his lack of trust in her judgement, Catriona said acidly, 'Well, that's certainly not a charge that could be aimed at you, is it? Everyone knows you're too mean to spend a penny you don't have to.'

There was a sudden, taut silence in the car and Catriona waited, her heart beating fast, wondering if she'd gone too far. 'So that's what you think, is it?' Lucas said shortly.

'You asked for it,' she shot back, still angry. 'Why can't you leave me alone instead of——?'

Lucas suddenly swung the car off the road and slammed on the brakes, so violently that the engine cut out and Catriona was thrown against him. Before she could recover he turned and grabbed hold of her arms. Blazingly angry, he shook her, his fingers pressing into her skin, then said through gritted teeth, 'And you damn well asked for this.' His hand moved to her throat and for a stunned moment she thought he was going to throttle her, but then his head came down and Lucas took her mouth in bruising, hungry passion.

CHAPTER SIX

IT WAS a kiss like no other Catriona had ever received. She wasn't exactly inexperienced when it came to kissing, and had known passion, eagerness, and even something close to adoration. But never before had she been subjected to an indomitable will that steam-rollered over any resistance, overpowered her senses and compulsively demanded her reciprocation. Her air of fragility made men handle her with care and gentleness, not seize her in their arms and crush her against them, not hold her so tightly that she could hardly breathe, nor take her lips with such hunger that she reeled under the impact.

It was such a shock that she felt dizzy and light-headed, her mind in a whirl. I ought to be fighting him off, she told herself, but didn't attempt to. This isn't my style, she thought, but stayed quiescent in his hold. I should be angry, furious, I know that. So why am I just letting him do this? Why can't I feel anything but his mouth on mine? And this heat? And this swirling sensation, as if I'm in a whirlpool and being pulled down and down, as if I'm drowning, drowning in his kiss?

Catriona was hardly aware of it when Lucas let her go. Her senses were still spinning, as if she'd drunk too much wine and it had gone to her head. She stared at him, wide-eyed, not knowing whether she'd responded to his kiss or not. He was watching her closely, a frown between his brows, his breathing unsteady.

'Well?' he demanded.

It was that one short word that brought Catriona back to her senses. *What the hell does he expect?* she thought on a rush of indignation. *That I'm going to swear undying love to him after one kiss? Does the arrogant fool think I'm going to go all dewy-eyed and beg him to take me to bed, or something?* 'Well what?' she shot back at him acidly.

Lucas sighed. 'I guessed you'd be a hard case.' Then he reached out and kissed her again!

This time she fully intended to resist, and did in fact hold herself stiffly and put her hands against his chest. But Lucas merely laughed against her mouth and pulled her closer to him, his shoulders hunching as he kissed her even more deeply than before.

It hadn't been surprise or shock the first time; again Catriona found herself in an erotic maelstrom, his arrant desire sweeping her down into a vortex of abandoned euphoria. But this time it was different, because deep inside herself she felt a growing ache, an insidious urge to respond, a need to be even closer to him. It was an urge that Catriona recognised in time as desire, and frightened her into action. She began to struggle, closing her mouth and turning her head in sudden panic. Lucas made a sound of angry protest and put his hand behind her head, holding her still. Immediately she bit his lip, and used all her strength to push him an inch or two away.

'Damn you! Let go of me.'

He released her at once and Catriona shrank back against the side of the car, her arms instinctively going across her chest. Lucas, his voice thick, said on a taunting note, 'What's the matter, Catriona? What are you afraid of?'

Fear, and a desperate attempt at self-preservation made her say, 'Afraid? Well, it certainly isn't of you!' And she laughed contemptuously.

'Why fight me off, then? Especially when you were really beginning to enjoy it.'

'Nonsense! Why, you don't even know how to kiss a girl!'

'No?'

'No! You make me feel as if I've been mauled by a bear.'

An amused glint came into his eyes. 'Maybe you'd better give me some lessons, then. I'm sure I'd make a very attentive pupil.'

'Oh, for heaven's sake! And you had the nerve to warn me against Omar!'

Lucas's face immediately hardened. 'Maybe you prefer his kisses,' he said jeeringly. 'I suppose he's gentle and undemanding. Treats you like some delicate flower.'

'I wouldn't know,' Catriona said shortly. 'He hasn't kissed me yet.'

'No? Didn't he kiss you goodbye tonight? It certainly looked like it.'

'Well, you're wrong.' She gave an angry sigh. 'Couldn't you see that he staged all that for your benefit? Giving me the money, whispering something in my ear; it was all meant to make you angry.'

'Angry—or jealous?'

Unsteadily she said, 'You have no reason to be jealous—nor any right to be, either. I'm not interested in Omar, and I'm certainly not interested in *you*. All I want is to be left alone to get on with my job.'

'That may be what you say you want, Catriona, but you're not immune to me; I've found out that at least tonight.'

Her cheeks flushed—not only by anger—and, her eyes sparking defiance, she said tersely, 'Don't kid yourself. You may have gone over big with innocent little girls right out of college, but I'm not so easily taken in—and I'm certainly not impressed by the macho caveman act.

You're not my type, Lucas; I like a man who's civilised, who knows how to treat a woman and make her feel good. Do you really think you've only got to kiss me—if you can call that sledge-hammer attack a kiss—and I'm going to fall apart at your feet? You must be mad!'

Lucas was watching her intently, his eyes fixed on her face. Slowly, almost to himself, he said, 'Yes, I think you're right; maybe I am mad.'

Suddenly uneasy, Catriona said impatiently, 'Look, just start the car again, will you? I want to get to the house.'

'All right, if that's really what you want.'

'Yes, it is.'

'Pity; I thought we might drive into Luxor and take a stroll beside the river.'

She knew he'd only said it to tease her, but got her revenge by saying, 'Is that usually where you take your dates for a big night out? Maybe you even splash out and buy them a cake from one of the stalls.'

'One of these days,' Lucas said softly, his eyes narrowed, 'I'm going to make you apologise for that remark.'

But at least he started the car and drove them the rest of the way home.

As soon as the Land Rover stopped at the house, Catriona got out and went to stride inside, then remembered her parcel and went back for it. She started to lug it out, but Lucas came round the car and said, 'Here, let me do it.'

'I can manage, thanks,' she said shortly, deliberately not looking at him.

'Don't be silly.'

Lucas went to reach past her, but she rounded on him angrily. 'I said I can do it!' Then, making a furious gesture of dismissal, she said, 'Oh, to hell with it!'

Turning on her heel, she ran inside and straight up to her room.

Leaning her elbows on the chest of drawers, Catriona put her head in her hands and found that she was still trembling. With anger? Yes, of course, what else? Or was it because Lucas was right and she really was afraid—not of him but of the effect that kiss had had on her? Slowly she lifted her head and gazed in the mirror. Her cheeks were still flushed and her eyes wide and apprehensive. What a fuss over a kiss, she thought. But it was impossible to dismiss it from her mind. With anyone else she would have known that a kiss was emotive of desire, of attraction. But she found it impossible to be certain with Lucas. He might have done it because he thought Omar had kissed her and wanted to show her what he could do in comparison. Or merely because it had amused him. Or because he routinely seduced all the women who came to work in his team.

That last thought left a nasty taste in her mouth. She had been right to fight him off, right to subjugate that surge of desire that she'd felt in his arms, a feeling so strong that she was still shaking from it. In future she must be doubly on her guard, Catriona warned herself, because to fall for Lucas would be fatal. He was an unfeeling, mean chauvinist, and the further she kept away from him, the better.

Quickly now, she washed herself and brushed her hair, put on a thin nightdress and got into bed. Then sat up with a jerk! Unable to believe it, she jumped out again and pulled the sheet aside to stare down at the mattress. A brand-new smooth and cushioned mattress! No lumps, no bare patches where the springs could dig into you, no stains where previous occupants had spilt drinks. Catriona was so surprised that for a moment she couldn't think, then it dawned on her that it had to be Lucas who had got it for her. And she had just accused him of being mean and miserly, when all the time . . . ! And he hadn't said anything, hadn't thrown his gesture back at her, which he easily could have done. Which a lesser man might have done.

Sitting down on the bed, Catriona ran her hand over the mattress, trying to think. Her first instinct was to rush to thank him for the gift, but she hesitated because now that he'd kissed her things were different between them, and she was afraid it might be misinterpreted. But she certainly ought to apologise for thinking him mean.

A knock, a rap from firm knuckles, made her jump. Instinctively she knew it was Lucas.

'Just a minute.' Quickly she pulled on her bath robe and opened the door.

His eyes flicked over her, noted her loose hair and the way it softened her face. 'Your parcel,' he said, and came in to put it on the floor. Straightening up, he glanced towards the bed and saw that it had been disturbed, but his face gave nothing away.

He went to walk out of the room but she said, 'Lucas—thanks.'

'It was no trouble.'

'No, I don't mean for the parcel. I meant for the mattress. It was—very kind of you.' He shrugged and she said, 'And I'm sorry, for what I said.'

'You said a lot of things.'

'You—made me angry.'

'Did I?' His eyes were on her now, with a strangely intent look in their grey depths. The sort of look a man got in his eyes when he's contemplating kissing you. Catriona's breath caught in her throat and she grew very still, but then he gave a rather rueful smile and he said, 'I disturbed you, I'm sorry. I'll let you get to sleep.'

'And tonight I really will sleep—thanks to you.'

But he shrugged off her thanks and went out, firmly closing the door behind him. Catriona stood staring after him, thinking that she'd been proved wrong in one aspect of his character, but that didn't mean that she hadn't been right in others. She must go on holding him at a distance—because if he'd kissed her again just now it might not have been so easy to resist.

Guessing that if she asked Lamia to get the servants to paint the room for her it would never get done, Catriona decided to do the job herself. As soon as she got home from the dig the next day, she got Mike to give her a hand to pull out all the furniture, then set to work, first to wash the ceiling. It was so uneven that it would have made a good plasterer cry, but that she could do little about.

Mike stood in the doorway watching. 'You really know how to do that, don't you?' he said admiringly.

Catriona was standing on a rather rickety stepladder, a scarf tied over her hair, and wearing an old shirt, the sleeves rolled up, and a pair of shorts. 'Of course. Don't you?'

'No, my mother always had the decorators in to do everything.'

'I'll show you how, if you like,' she offered generously.

Mike laughed. 'Nice try.' And he went away.

The servants were the next to come and stand in the doorway to watch. Catriona was afraid they might resent her doing the job instead of them, but the huge grins on their faces told her they were only too pleased not to have the bother. A command in Egyptian sent them scurrying away and Lamia appeared in the doorway.

'What on earth are you doing?'

'Painting my room.'

'Did Lucas tell you to do this?'

'No, of course not.'

Lamia stared at her, not knowing what to say, but couldn't resist a vehement, 'You're mad!' before she walked away, her high heels clicking on the tiled floor.

'What the hell?' An exclamation outside in the corridor an hour or so later gave her warning of Lucas's presence. 'What's all this stuff doing out here?' He walked through the doorway, stopped, and put his hands on his hips as he looked up at her. 'Just what do you think you're doing?'

Catriona sighed exasperatedly. 'Why does everybody ask that? What does it look like? I'm redecorating my room, of course. Why is it so amazing?'

'Probably because no one has ever done it before. Where did you get the paint?' he asked, touching a tin with his foot.

'I bought it in Luxor, yesterday,' she answered coolly.

'Did you, indeed? Was that what was in the parcel you brought back from Omar's place?'

'Yes.'

Things obviously clicked into place because Lucas said, 'And I suppose that was what you wanted your wages for?' Catriona didn't bother to answer because it was none of his business. But her silence made Lucas give an angry exclamation, reach up to put his hands round her waist and easily set her down on the floor. But he kept his hands on her as he said, 'I can't stand women who sulk. Did you or did you not buy the paint out of your wages?'

'Yes, if you must know.'

'Why didn't you ask me for the money to buy it?' he demanded.

Catriona's shirt was hanging loose over her shorts, and when he'd got hold of her he'd put his hands under the shirt, so now she could feel his warmth and strength against her bare skin. It unnerved her and she pushed him away. 'Because I was told—I mean I didn't think that you would give it to me.'

He gave her a sharp look. 'Who told you?'

'No one. It was just what I thought,' she lied, feeling terrible now because he'd bought her the mattress. To change the subject she resorted to impatience. 'I must get on; I'm trying to get this ceiling finished while it's still light.'

'Do you need any help?'

'From you?' she asked in surprised disbelief.

His mouth twisted at her tone. 'No, from Aly.'

She laughed shortly, implying that was the answer she'd expected, but then said, 'He can give me a hand to put the furniture back when I've finished tonight, if that's OK?'

'How long is it going to take you to entirely finish the room?'

'About a week, I suppose.'

'And do you intend to move the furniture in and out every time you work on it? And are you going to sleep in a room full of paint fumes?'

'I don't have any choice,' Catriona pointed out.

'I don't suppose you even thought of that aspect of it. Women seldom think things through; they just get excited about an idea and decide to go ahead with it,' he remarked disparagingly.

'All right,' Catriona said in annoyed challenge. 'What do you suggest?'

'I think you'd better move into Harry Carson's room until you've finished.'

'Harry Carson? Oh, the pottery man who's on leave. Will he mind?'

'He isn't here to object,' Lucas stated with cold logic. 'Well?'

'Yes, it's a good idea. Thanks.'

'Get Aly to help you move your stuff.'

Later that evening she collected her personal belongings and took them across the landing to the room that Aly had made ready for her. She hadn't been sure which one it was, but when he opened the door to usher her in, she saw that it was the room next door to Lucas's. The mud walls in the house weren't thick enough to cut out noise; as Catriona lay in the new bed, complete with her new mattress which she was determined to guard with her life, she realised that Lucas's bed must be just a few inches away on the other side of the partition wall. She heard him moving around and the scrape of a chair on the bare floor. She fancied that she could even hear him breathing, and was tempted to say goodnight, but resisted it. After the way he'd kissed her, Catriona supposed that she ought to be nervous of being so close to him, with no one to see him if he slipped inside. For half an hour she lay there, listening intently, but as soon as she heard the creak of the wooden slats as he got into bed she fell asleep and didn't worry about it again while she used the room.

It took nearly all her free time that week to finish painting the room, and in the meantime she'd borrowed a sewing-machine from Mrs Aziz and, during her free time at the Garden of the Nile, had made the curtains for the window. On Friday evening Aly helped her carry the furniture back in and she looked at the room with some satisfaction. At least now it looked clean and bright; the basics were there, although a great deal could still be done to it. Stencilling or some other paint effect would look good on the walls, and the furniture could also stand being painted.

She went down to supper feeling tired but content. Only Mike and Lucas were there, and they mostly talked about the results of some DNA tests that had been done on a mummified body belonging to a museum, highly technical stuff. But afterwards Lucas lent her a book showing some of the best wall paintings to be found in Egypt. Fascinated by the costumes worn by the figures, Catriona sat at a table with a drawing-pad and amused herself by updating the ancient Egyptian dress and giving it a modern look. There were definite possibilities, especially with the totally pleated dresses.

It was Saturday the next day, which was lucky because Catriona slept late and would never have made it in time to go to the dig. As it was she was only just ready when Omar's car arrived to collect her. She had been so busy during the week that she had forgotten about Omar's planned surprise, but he had again stayed on another day at the house and told her that he was going to take them that night to see the *son et lumière* at Karnak. 'So you should telephone Dr Kane and tell him that you will be late and my chauffeur will bring you back,' Omar told her.

Catriona did so but Lucas wasn't there, so she left a message with Aly. Often, when Lucas was driving her home and he went through the town, she had seen the crowds of people who waited outside the entrance to the temples every night for the *son et lumière* performances. These lasted for almost two hours and there were usually two a night, in different languages, but in summer, when there were fewer tourists, only one. She supposed that tonight there would be an English performance, around seven-thirty. But the girls, together with Catriona, were allowed to have dinner with their father that evening and they didn't eat until eight, so it wasn't until almost nine-thirty when they all got into the car and were driven into the town.

Maybe we're going to an Arabic performance, Catriona thought, but when they arrived at the great car park, which was usually full of coaches and cars, it was virtually empty and there was no one waiting outside. Omar must have got the time or the day wrong, Catriona thought with a sick feeling of disappointment on the girls' behalf. They got out of the car at the entrance and walked down the avenue of wide, shallow steps between the crouching statues of the sphinx. Two men came to greet them, the doors leading to the precinct were opened and they all went inside, then the doors were shut again. Catriona turned to look at Omar, her eyes wide in astonishment.

He smiled, enjoying her amazement, and said, 'I thought we would have a private performance. So much better for the children than being dwarfed and pushed by the crowds, don't you think?'

Catriona nodded dumbly, took hold of the girls' hands and followed him and the guide into the entrance way of the temple. Music sounded in the background, then voices began to tell the story of Karnak, lights played on the ruins and drew them in further. They came to the great temple of Amun, the huge columns towering high into the sky, outlined against the moon. The girls, overawed, had slid away to clutch their father's hands, so Catriona was able to reach out to gently touch the warm stone of one of the columns and felt the nearest she had ever come to history. The recorded voices and music took them through the temple, on through the darkened ruins and to a long terrace of tiered seats facing the sacred lake, seats that the audience normally filled. They sat on the front row, in the middle, and listened to the rest of the performance as the voices brought them forward through the thousands of years of history and myth. They heard the clash of steel and the drumming hoofs of charging horses, watched as the lights played on columns and carved walls, on obelisk and statue.

The girls had sat in ecstatic silence, listening to Omar's whispered translation, but as soon as the last note of music came to an end threw themselves at him to thank him. He laughed, hugging them both, enjoying their pleasure. Then he looked over Dorreya's head at Catriona and raised an eyebrow. 'Did you not enjoy it?'

She smiled in polite gratitude. 'Of course. Thank you.'

'So don't I get a hug from you, too?'

She laughed, but shook her head.

Omar made a pouting face. 'And after I arranged all this to please you.' Immediately her face changed, became withdrawn, but Omar quickly remedied his slip and said, 'At least my daughters appreciate my efforts,' and saw Catriona relax again.

They walked slowly back to the car, the girls too excited to speak English and chattering away to their father as they held his hands. Catriona followed, pleased that the girls had enjoyed themselves so much. They all sat in the back of the big car, as they had on the outward journey.

'The girls are tired so we'll drop them off first,' Omar remarked as they drove back to the Garden of the Nile.

She was lost in thought and the casual remark almost slipped by her, but then Catriona sat up. '"We"?' she questioned.

'Yes,' Omar answered imperturbably. 'I cannot let you travel alone at this time of night.'

'I'm sure I'll be quite safe with your chauffeur.'

'He does not count,' Omar stated with aristocratic indifference. 'He is merely a servant.'

Catriona gasped, momentarily stunned by his arrogance, then said shortly, 'But I work for you too, which puts me on a level with him.'

'Nonsense, it is quite different.'

'I wouldn't want to put you to any inconvenience,' she said stiffly.

Omar smiled. 'You are angry with me. You have been taught that all people are equal, but in your mind you know that is not true. And this is Egypt; here we accept reality. So, please, do not argue any more. Surely you would rather I escorted you home?'

Catriona was quite sure she wouldn't, but he was obviously determined so there was no point in protesting further. Anyway, she would be safe enough with the chauffeur there; he counted with her even if he didn't with Omar.

But when they reached the Garden of the Nile and she'd handed two very sleepy little girls over to Mrs Aziz, Catriona went back to the car and found that Omar had dismissed the chauffeur.

'It's such a pleasant evening; I thought I'd drive you myself.' And he opened the front passenger door for her.

Hesitating on the last step, Catriona said, 'I thought you said the chauffeur was coming with us?'

Leaning his arms on the top of the door, Omar gave her an amused look. 'You always seem so afraid of me.'

'Not afraid, just cautious.'

'Good, you should be cautious, especially when you're with Dr Kane. But, Catriona,' he gave her a reproachful look, 'have I not kept my promise? Have I ever given you reason to be wary of me? Have I not treated you with respect, as I would any female guest in my house? I am not the kind of man who sees a woman, wants her, and who immediately and rudely tries to get her.' He frowned. 'You have an expression in English for it, but I can't remember...'

'Making a pass?' Catriona suggested.

'No, it is more explicit than that.'

'Oh. You mean, coming on heavy.'

He nodded. 'Yes. A very boorish phrase to describe boorish behaviour. But I am a very civilised man, Catriona, and would not dream of distressing you in any way. You may trust me. You have my promise.'

She didn't entirely believe him, but without further argument Catriona got into the car.

Omar didn't drive as well as his chauffeur, didn't in fact seem to be all that familiar with the controls, but it was well past midnight and there was little traffic about in a country where most people got up at daybreak. It

was the first time that she had been completely alone
with Omar and, despite his reassurances, Catriona didn't
feel completely at ease. Probably because Lucas had told
her not to trust him. But then she wasn't at all sure that
she could trust Lucas either.

Not liking that train of thought, Catriona said quickly,
'I understand that your family goes back a long way,
that you were once aristocrats in Egypt?'

It was the right thing to say; Omar became eloquent
as he unfolded his family history which he could trace
back with certainty over a thousand years. He told her
of ancestors who had fought against the Mamelukes and
the Ottomans, of another who had met Napoleon, and
yet another who had been a courtier at the court of
Farouk, the last King of Egypt. 'But now we are a re-
public, which is much better for the country,' he finished.

'And what do you do?'

'I am a businessman. I have many interests here and
abroad.'

It was a vague answer, and Catriona guessed that it
wasn't a subject he wished to discuss, especially with a
woman. He didn't in turn ask her about her family, she
noticed, but went on to talk about Cairo, ending by
telling her that she must see it.

'I'm looking forward to doing so. Lucas has said that
he'll fix it for me to go to the museum.'

Omar gave a disparaging wave of his hand. 'There is
much more to Cairo than the museum. Do you find
Egypt interesting?'

'Very much so.'

'I'm glad.' He switched on the main beams as they
drove through the quiet village of Mem Habu near the
excavation site, then gave her a sideways glance. 'And
do you find *me* interesting?' he asked in a tone that
implied it was a foregone conclusion, that she must
find him so.

'Of course,' she agreed dutifully.

'That, too, makes me glad. Because I find that *you* interest me extremely, Catriona.'

She groaned inwardly, having expected this. 'Really?' she answered, putting as much coldness as she could into the word.

Pulling up outside the excavation house, Omar took her literally and said, 'Yes, I really do.' She reached for the door-handle but he put a hand on her arm. 'So what is your reaction?'

But Catriona ducked that one. 'I'm too tired to have any reaction—and I have to get up at five; that's only four hours away.'

'If you came to teach the girls full-time, you would not have to get up so early,' he said persuasively.

'No, thanks. I'm happy with things as they are.'

'You are a very independent young lady. I haven't met a woman like you before.' She reached for the handle a second time, but he said quickly, 'No, let me do that,' and came round to open the door for her.

'Goodnight. Thank you for a wonderful evening,' Catriona said politely, eager to get away from him.

'Goodnight.' To her dismay Omar took her hand and lightly kissed it. 'Tonight has been wonderful for me, also.'

She watched him drive away, even the low noise of the Mercedes' engine echoing through the stillness of the desert, then turned and walked towards the house. Lucas straightened up from where he'd been leaning against the doorway. 'It seems a wonderful time was had by all,' he mocked.

'Have you been waiting up for me?'

'I thought the chauffeur was supposed to be bringing you home.'

'Omar changed his mind.'

'Oh, I don't think he changed it; he had it in mind from the beginning. Where did he take you?'

'To Karnak. Back into the past.'

Putting his hands on her waist, Lucas drew her to him. 'How into the past?'

'To the *son et lumière*.'

'What?' He gave a short laugh of derision. 'You call that wonderful? Canned music and potted, sentimentalised history for a crowd of tourists!'

'It was very interesting to see the ruins in the moonlight,' Catriona said stiffly, mentally agreeing with him but determined not to let him see it.

Lucas's hands tightened on her waist. 'The *son et lumière* ended hours ago; where have you been since then?'

Shaking her head, Catriona said, 'No, we were the only ones there. Omar arranged a private performance, for just the four of us.'

'So was it the ruins—or the power of money that's gone to your head?' Lucas said sneeringly.

'Nothing has gone to my head. It was an interesting experience, that's all.' Her eyes grew reflective. 'The ruins were magnificent, though. They're the first I've seen in Egypt, and to see them in those circumstances was certainly something.'

'You're easily pleased, Catriona.' Lucas's voice was rough, almost angry.

She shrugged. 'Possibly. But it was something to remember.'

'Karnak to recorded music and cheap lighting effects!' he said in disgust. 'It deserves better than that.' He gave her a long, brooding look, something obviously on his mind, but then, almost abstractedly, bent to kiss her neck. A *frisson* of sensuality ran through her and she tilted her head as he kissed the long column of her throat.

His lips found hers and Catriona put her arms round his neck, her mouth opening under his as Lucas held her close, his body hard against her own. There was no abstraction about him now, his lips were eager, demanding. She felt desire take hold, was tempted to surrender to it, but moved away and stepped out of his arms.

She laughed and evaded him when he went to pull her back again, her heart suddenly dancing. 'Goodnight, Lucas.'

He made no further attempt to restrain her, instead putting his hands in his pockets and leaning back against the wall. His eyes slightly mocking, he said. 'How's the mattress—comfortable?'

'Very.'

He grinned. 'I'm tempted to try it myself.'

Catriona turned her head so that he couldn't see her smile, and merely said again, 'Goodnight, Lucas.'

'Sweet dreams,' he answered on a soft, teasing note, sure now that if she dreamed at all it would be of him.

But Catriona slept soundly, waking only when the alarm clock went off, and rushing downstairs to join the others for breakfast. Lucas drove them to the dig, stayed there for a few hours, then went off somewhere, but he was back in time to drive them all back to the house at the end of the day.

'I bought enough paint to redecorate the sitting-room,' Catriona told him on the way. 'Is it OK if I start today?'

'Sounds a great idea—but we'll all lend a hand,' he added, raising his voice.

Behind them, Bryan and Mike groaned, but Mohamed didn't say anything, and when they'd had their meal and started moving all the furniture out of the sitting-room, he and Lamia went out.

'They obviously aren't into decorating,' Catriona commented as she watched through the window as they drove away.

'This isn't a land of do-it-yourself, but of have-someone-to-do-it-for-you,' Lucas told her. 'Labour is cheap and people need the work. But we need this room, so the job has to be done quickly.' But Catriona noticed that he got Aly and a couple of the site workmen in to help and they got the room finished that night.

There was still some white paint on her hair when she went to Omar's house the next morning. He had gone back to Cairo, but the girls noticed, so at lunchtime Catriona went up to the room where she'd once slept and which she now regarded as her own, to wash it out. In the bathroom there was a plentiful supply of shampoos and cosmetics bearing the best known brand names in the world. Her hair gleamed like molten metal when she'd dried it and whirled into a soft golden mane when she tossed her head. Afterwards Catriona put on a swimsuit and glanced at herself in the mirror. I'm becoming sleek, working here, she thought, looking at her tanned skin and soft, rounded curves. She had been too thin when she'd arrived in Egypt, the result of living off cheap food for months, but Mrs Aziz loved little rich cakes and the cook at the Garden of the Nile was expert at making them. So now Catriona was like a sleek, contented cat, with a light of excitement in her eyes.

Stretched out by the pool to sunbathe, she thought about that excitement. Part of it, she decided, must be from simple youth and joy of life, from doing a job that she loved and being in a strange country. But that was only a small part and definitely not the most important. She considered herself to be an adult, not an impressionable teenager, and past the stage of heady excitement that sexual attraction brought. Boyfriends had mostly proved to be a disappointment, either having nothing but sex on their minds, or thinking more of themselves than the girl they were with. There had been a couple of young men whom she'd gone steady with, but when she'd thought about being their unpaid servant for life—and being available for sex whenever they wanted it—the attraction had swiftly palled.

Both Lucas and Omar were older than most of the men she knew, and she guessed that they were both fully experienced when it came to women. And they both seemed to be fascinated by her, which was an aphrodisiac in itself. Although very different types, it would seem that they both wanted her, but had very different ways of going about it. There was no question as to which she preferred, of course—Omar just didn't come into it. It was Lucas who continually filled her thoughts, but it was interesting to compare the two, if only to underline all the things about Lucas that she found so attractive: his self-assurance and rugged good looks, his strong masculinity that did crazy things to her libido.

Catriona sighed and turned over on to her front, reminding herself that her career was more important to her than any man. It was a resolution she'd made after the last romantic disappointment, nearly a year ago now, and so far she'd kept it. But now... Was either man to be taken seriously? Maybe they were just amusing themselves, or else each trying to score off the other. The thought made her uneasy, unsure of Lucas. Again she resolved to be wary, to not let herself fall for him; that could well be a fatal thing to do.

On Thursday evening there was a party to celebrate someone's birthday over at the French excavation house, and they all went along. The food was good, there was plenty of wine to drink, and they had a record player to which they were soon all dancing. As there were far more men than women, Catriona was popular and was on her feet most of the night, dancing with whoever asked her. Lucas didn't dance all that much, but in the early hours of the morning, when the music had become slow and smoochy, he came over to where Catriona was sitting, pulled her to her feet, put both arms round her and began to move with the beat.

They were out in the open, in the French courtyard. Coloured lights had been strung up and light shone through the open windows, creating a circle of brightness and conviviality out of the night. Lucas did not hold her tightly, but there was possessiveness in the way he'd put his arms round her and had taken it for granted that she wanted to dance with him. Resting her hands lightly on his shoulders, Catriona said, 'I suppose you've been talking shop.'

'At a party? Now would I?'

She chuckled. 'Of course you would. Archaeology is the love of your life, isn't it?'

'Perhaps. I admit no other love has emerged to rival it—yet.'

'Yet?' she couldn't resist asking.

'One never knows what may come along in the future.'

'Not *who* may come along?'

'There is always that possibility, of course.'

'But not one you expect?'

'An archaeologist never "expects" to find anything; he just makes what he can of what comes along.'

He was fencing with her, she knew, giving enigmatic answers that she could take which way she liked. Catriona gave a small sigh. 'It's too late for all this verbal repartee. I'm too tired to be witty.'

'Tired? I hope not.'

'It's almost three in the morning,' Catriona pointed out. 'I'm entitled to be tired.'

'Then you'd better wake up, because we're going out.'

'Out!' She stared at him. 'Where? When?'

'Now.' Taking her hand, Lucas shouted a goodbye to everyone and walked her over to the Land Rover.

'Hey, wait a minute,' she protested, 'I haven't said thanks for the party.'

He pushed her in the car and got in beside her. 'You can send them a note tomorrow.'

'What about the others; how are they going to get home?'

'Someone will give them a lift, if they bother to go home at all.'

'Where are we going?'

But he wouldn't tell her, just drove along the dark, quiet roads.

'Wake up. We're here.'

Catriona stirred, and found that she'd fallen asleep with her head resting against Lucas's shoulder. Quickly straightening up, she looked out of the window and saw that they were at Karnak. She gave Lucas a puzzled look, but he was already getting out of the car. They walked up to the gate, a man appeared but no money changed hands before the gate was opened for them to go through.

It was very dark inside. Catriona reached for Lucas and his hand closed round hers, warm, reassuring. 'I don't understand,' she said in a whisper. 'Why have you brought me here again?'

'You'll see. Come on.'

There was no music, no floodlights making the ruins bright as day, not even a guide with a torch, but Lucas seemed to know his way and led her unerringly along. He came to a stop and she knew that she was in the hypostyle hall of the Great Temple of Amun, was aware of the stone forest of huge papyrus-crowned columns all around her. Lucas let her go, moved away from her, and for a moment Catriona felt fear, but then his voice came softly out of the darkness and began to tell her of the boy king Tutankhamun who had come this way to his coronation, of the priests and court nobles who had led him in, a small child of nine walking beneath these great columns. Of the musicians who had played for him, their music echoing among the stones as the great procession moved slowly on into the inner temple and into the presence of Amun, the god of gods. 'Close your eyes,' he murmured. 'Don't you hear the drum and the lute, and the reed pipes?'

Lucas began to recite poetry to her, some in the original Egyptian, some that she could understand. Phrases danced in her mind: 'Lord of the thrones of the two lands', 'The sun god', 'enduring forever'. And then a poem she'd heard before, but never like this, never with such meaning and such truth.

> 'And on the pedestal these words appear:
> "My name is Ozymandias, king of kings:
> Look on my works, ye mighty, and despair!"'

There was silence as the words died away, then Lucas's voice again, 'Open your eyes, Catriona. Look up.'

She did so and saw the first rays of dawn breaking through the sky, saw the rich golden light touch the heads of the columns and bring to life the brilliant colours that still adorned them. She caught her breath as carved muscles seemed to flex, eyes to see, and mouths to smile, welcoming the new day. The sun rose and the temple filled with glorious light, became again the temple of worship that it was created to be, reached out for the dawn's aubade and, as it had done for thousands of years, became the greatest monument that man had ever made to their gods.

She stood and stared until the sun parted from the horizon, until the sky was completely blue, the glory of the dawn forever reaching out to another land. Her heart felt that it would burst with the wonder of it and tears ran down Catriona's cheeks. She turned to Lucas but was unable to speak. Putting his arm round her, he led her out into the wakening town, to the car and home.

CHAPTER SEVEN

CATRIONA sat silently in the Land Rover on the way home, almost unaware of her surroundings, of the growing number of cyclists and pedestrians, of the buses overflowing with people, all making their way to work in the town. Her eyes and mind were still full of the radiance of the dawn, of Lucas's voice in the darkness, speaking prayer and praise, but ending on that note of might and majesty. And what magnificent relics those ancient people had left for modern man to wonder at!

The *son et lumière* performance that Omar had taken her to had been momentarily exciting, but that excitement had been as nothing compared to the wonder that Lucas had given her. In fact, now that she came to think about it, Catriona wondered if half the excitement hadn't been the stirring quality of the music, the beat of drums and the heady summons of the trumpet. The noise of battle and the shouting voices had all added to the brief stimulation of the senses engendered by the performance. But that was all it had been, really, just a performance put on for the tourists, which anyone who paid could go and see whenever they wished. OK, so Omar had given them the show to themselves, but millions of others must already have seen it.

But this morning... Catriona's heart ached with the remembered beauty of it. Never had she imagined that Lucas would take her to a place that she'd already seen and show her what history could really mean, make the *son et lumière* seem so flat and contrived in comparison.

138

They reached the edge of the desert and she turned for the first time to look at him.

'Recovered?' he asked, glancing at her.

Catriona smiled and nodded. 'Thanks for taking me. It was one of the most unforgettable experiences of my life.'

'Really?' He raised a quizzical eyebrow.

Catriona realised that he was teasing her and smiled. 'Really,' she said with sincerity.

'There are plenty more places like that in Egypt. That's why I love the country so much.'

Teasing in return, she said, 'You think we should give back the Sphinx's beard?'

Lucas grinned. 'Definitely.'

Catriona leaned her head back against the seat, looking out into the desert, always at its best at this time in the morning. She should have felt tired out after a night almost entirely devoid of sleep, but she was still wide awake. To sleep, she thought, would mean losing some of the miracle of the morning, and she didn't want to lose any of it, ever, especially when it was still so close, so incredibly dazzling in her mind.

But when they reached the house, Lucas said, 'You should go to bed, get some sleep.'

'I'm not tired. I feel—oh, I don't know, just too *full* to go to bed. I want to do something, go somewhere.' She made a restless movement. 'Don't you understand? You were there too; surely you feel the same way?'

He shook his head and turned off the engine. 'I have some work to do.'

'You don't have to work; it's Friday.'

'I've some reports I have to catch up on.'

An unwelcome thought occurred to her, making Catriona say tightly, 'I suppose you've seen Karnak at dawn before, so the novelty has worn off.'

'Yes, I have,' he agreed. 'But nothing, even if you went there every morning of the year, could detract from it.'

'But you must have taken other girls there often, and——'

'No,' Lucas interrupted. 'You're the only person I've ever shared it with.' His eyes held hers. 'Ever wanted to share it with.' Leaning forward, he kissed her gently on the mouth, a lingering kiss that demanded nothing, but even so stirred her soul. When he drew away Catriona opened her eyes very languorously, as if the lids were incredibly heavy. 'Is that what you want?' Lucas asked softly. 'Is that the way you want to finish the night?'

She gazed into his face, trying to read his thoughts, his feelings, but then sighed and shook her head a little. 'No—I don't know.'

Strangely, that made him smile. 'I must be losing my touch.' He sat back. 'Go and get some sleep,' he ordered, his voice normal again.

They got out of the car and went into the house, Lucas going straight into the finds room. Catriona moved towards the stairs, but then, still too restless, turned and went into the main room. Sitting at the table underneath the window, she began to play around again with ideas for clothes based on ancient wall paintings, but her mind was too full and her attention soon wandered. It was impossible to deny to herself any longer that she was greatly attracted to Lucas. He was a very vital, masculine man, and it would have been easy to say yes to him this morning. But sex just to round off a most unusual night and dawn? No way! *That* certainly wasn't what she wanted.

So what did she want? That was harder to answer. Maybe she wasn't even sure yet herself. But perhaps what she wanted didn't come into it; what Lucas wanted might not be the same. Catriona tried to look at this objectively. No one had actually said so, but she had got the impression that Lucas was a bit of a playboy where women were concerned. There was her predecessor, Elaine, who had gone back to England because she was pregnant. Mike hadn't said for certain that Lucas was responsible, but on the other hand he hadn't denied it either. Then there was Lamia, who liked to captivate the men around her, and who definitely had an eye for Lucas when her husband wasn't in the room. So did Lucas, then, have an eye for women as Lamia had for men? Was he just amusing himself with her, Catriona? Was she there and so he had to try and win her over, make love to her, and then discard her for the next girl who came along? Or was he, as she'd suspected before, just out to get her because he thought Omar fancied her?

Such thoughts made Catriona feel angry and humiliated. Jumping to her feet, she was on the point of marching into the finds room and telling Lucas to keep away from her in future, but realised in time that doing so would tell him as clearly as words that he'd got under her skin. Pride forbade that. She stood still, hands clenched, then wondered why it mattered so much. She'd met enough men like that in the past, men who had no intention of settling down and who just wanted to sleep with as many girls as possible, to boast about, and to boost their narcissistic egos.

It came to her that she desperately didn't want Lucas to be that kind of man. Maybe he wasn't. Maybe she'd misjudged him. She just didn't know. He was single, but experienced; that ought to tell her something. He'd known other women but hadn't got entangled, so must be adept at handling relationships—or just at extracting himself from them. Catriona found her instincts were at war. Her heart wanted to trust him; her mind screamed, 'Beware!' Common sense at length came to her aid, and she realised that she had to keep him at a distance, to flirt with him, perhaps, but not to allow him to stir her emotions. That way, in time, she might find out whether or not he really cared about her at all, or whether he was like a mountaineer and she a mountain, to be conquered because she was there.

Gathering together her drawings, Catriona went up to her room and got into bed, but it was a long time before she went to sleep.

She didn't see Lucas again that day, but Omar was at home again when she went to the Garden of the Nile the next morning. To her surprise, he took her and the girls out to lunch with him to a restaurant in Luxor, and informed them that he'd decided to take a holiday to show her and the girls more of the ancient sites. The girls were agog with excitement but Catriona heard the news with dismay. She said, 'But you can't want me along? That is, it's very kind of you, but surely you'd rather be alone with your daughters?'

But they all, the girls especially, insisted she go along. Omar wanted her to choose where they would go, but she refused, not wanting to show any enthusiasm.

'Then I will choose,' Omar decreed. 'But you must please be here earlier on Monday. I will send the car for you at seven. And you will tell Dr Kane that my chauffeur will bring you home.'

'That's what I told him last time,' Catriona pointed out. 'But *you* drove me back; he may not believe you this time.'

Omar's lip curled in amusement. 'Did he wait for you to come home?'

'Yes.'

'Dear Dr Kane is behaving like an anxious parent—or a lover.' Omar gave her an assessing look but her face betrayed nothing. 'But no—I think not. Well, he will just have to wait and see again, won't he?'

The restaurant was in the fashionable part of Luxor. Near by was a jewellery shop, one of the many in the town. Omar said something in Arabic to the girls, who nodded eagerly. 'We just wish to go into this shop,' he said to Catriona, so she had no choice but to follow them in.

It was the girls who did the buying, consulting gravely with the jeweller. Catriona wandered round the shop, looking at reproduction Tutankhamun face masks, model pyramids, trays of gold charms, everything that a tourist might want to buy as a souvenir, until the girls had made their purchase and it had been wrapped. They drove back to the house and Omar went to his study. Only then did Nadia and Dorreya hand her the parcel and tell Catriona the present was for her. Catriona knew this was entirely Omar's idea, that in reality the gift was from him, but he had arranged it in such a way that it was impossible for her to refuse. To have done so would have deeply upset the little girls, who were looking up at her with such happy, trusting faces.

So Catriona accepted the gift with a great show of surprised pleasure, and opened the little parcel as the girls looked on with bright, expectant faces, getting as much excitement out of the giving as Catriona managed to show in receiving it. Inside was a gold neck-chain from which was suspended a gold ankh, the ancient Egyptian symbol for long life. Because the girls had chosen it themselves, Catriona was genuinely pleased. They insisted that she put it on at once and laughed aloud when she gave them an impulsive hug of thanks. Omar came to join them for the evening meal and was obviously amused at the subtle way he'd managed to give her a present.

Lucas didn't come to meet her that evening; he sent Bryan instead, because two men from the French team were at the house. They were still there, having coffee

in the sitting-room, when she arrived. Lamia was doing
her 'perfect hostess' act, and revelling in being the only
woman there, so Catriona got a glower from her when
she walked in with Bryan. Lucas looked towards her and
smiled, but Catriona merely gave him a passing nod as
she helped herself to coffee. She was aware that he raised
a questioning eyebrow, but she sat in a chair near the
table, turning it so that she wasn't directly facing him.
When the Frenchmen left she took the opportunity to
go to her room.

In the middle of the night a searing pain in her stomach
jerked her into wakefulness. Catriona gasped and headed
for the bathroom; went back to bed but lay in groaning
discomfort, beads of sweat damping her nightdress to
her body. Twice more she went to the bathroom before
she gave in to her worst fears and realised that she must
have caught the proverbial Egyptian stomach bug and
had better do something about it. Pulling her robe round
her, she went round the darkened landing to Lucas's door
and knocked lightly.

'Who is it?' His voice answered at once, as if he'd
been lying awake.

'Catriona,' she called softly, not wanting to wake the
others.

When he opened the door Lucas had pulled on a pair
of jeans but his chest was bare. He stood silhouetted
against the light in his room, and there was tension in
his body and face as he said, 'What is it? What do
you——?' He broke off as he saw her leaning against
the wall, noticed her flushed face. 'The bug?' he said in
swift understanding.

She nodded. 'Have you got something I can take?'

'Of course. Go back to your room; I'll bring it along.'

He joined her in less than five minutes and gave her
some tablets to take and a glass of cool mineral water
to wash them down. Sitting on the edge of the bed, he

said, 'It will take an hour or so to work. Then take another couple in four hours' time.'

'I'll be at the dig then,' she said weakly.

'No, you won't. You must stay in bed all tomorrow. And don't have anything to eat for twenty-four hours.'

She started to protest but felt so lousy that she didn't argue when he insisted.

'What have you eaten today?' Lucas asked, and put a hand on her hot forehead.

Catriona leaned back against the pillow. 'Omar took us to a restaurant in Luxor.'

Lucas didn't look at all pleased. 'And I suppose you ate a load of rich stuff that your stomach wasn't used to?'

She managed a weak smile. 'I thought if I could stand the food dished up here, I could stand anything.'

'I thought you were supposed to be going there to tutor the girls?'

'It's part of their education to go out and about. I could hardly refuse to go just because Omar was going.'

'Maybe you didn't want to refuse.'

'Oh, for heaven's sake!' Catriona sighed tiredly. She had been thinking of asking Lucas's advice about the projected trips that Omar had suggested, but that seemed impossible now. Goaded, she said, 'It's your fault; if you hadn't taken his money I wouldn't be working for him.'

'Wouldn't you? You didn't seem at all averse to the idea.'

'And you weren't at all averse to taking his money— even though you didn't need it. Why did you take it? Why didn't you refuse to let me work for him?' she demanded fretfully.

Lucas gave her a strangely intent look. 'Maybe I was waiting for you to refuse, to turn down his offer.'

She frowned. 'I don't understand.'

'If you had really disliked Omar nothing would have made you go and work for him, but you accepted, which proves that you weren't immune to him. And I think you're still susceptible to his money and position, even if not to his suave charm and his——'

'No, I'm not,' Catriona interrupted forcefully. 'You have no right to say that.'

'Then leave.'

'What?'

'You heard me; leave.'

'If I leave you'll have to give the money back,' she pointed out tartly.

He shrugged. 'So I'll give it back. Well? Can you bear to give up the Garden of the Nile? Give up Omar?'

Catriona stared at him, unable to fathom him out, wondering if this was some sort of test. A gripping pain in her stomach made her clench her teeth. Anger filled her that he could be so insensitive, ask her to make this kind of decision when she was feeling so ill. It made her stubborn and indignant, made her want to annoy him, so, glaring at Lucas, she said, 'No, I don't want to damn well leave. And I'm not going to. Now, will you please get out of here so that I can be ill in peace?'

Standing up, Lucas glared down at her in turn. 'It'll be a pleasure,' he said curtly.

Angry and resentful, Catriona did as she'd been told and stayed in bed all the next day, the boy Aly bringing her drinks from time to time. In the evening Lamia was sent up to see how she was but Lucas didn't come himself. By the following morning Catriona was completely recovered and starving hungry, so, after the others had left for the dig, she had some breakfast and got ready to go out. Still annoyed with Lucas, she merely left a message telling him not to collect her that evening.

The girls and Omar were already in the car when it arrived at the excavation house, and they drove straight to the airport where they caught a plane to Abu Simbel. Here, to save them from being covered by the waters of the Aswan High Dam, the Egyptians had painstakingly rebuilt the great temples of Rameses II. Catriona gazed in awe at the sixty-foot-high statues but she missed Lucas's voice in her ear, making the past come alive for her again.

From Abu Simbel they flew to Aswan to see the dam and ate at a hotel overlooking the Nile, where they watched the white-sailed feluccas glide along like great water birds, then took a ride in a horse-drawn carriage heavy with brass ornaments and jingling harness, down roads shaded by palm trees.

On the whole it was a good day, and one which was repeated every time Catriona went to the Garden of the Nile that week. Omar put himself out to give them a good time, the big limousine whisked them in air-conditioned comfort from site to site, guides were always waiting to escort them round tomb or temple, often keeping ordinary tourists waiting while they were taken round. A table was always booked at the best restaurant, and they were treated with what Catriona felt was obsequious attention. And Omar insisted on buying expensive souvenirs for the girls, and so of course for Catriona; she had to be careful not to admire something or he would buy it for her, even though she tried to refuse. He began to touch her a lot more, too, taking her hand unnecessarily to help her up steps and not letting go immediately as they walked along until she pulled away.

Nadia and Dorreya enjoyed their trips, which pleased Catriona, but she couldn't help wondering whether Omar would have bothered to organise them if he hadn't wanted to impress her. He didn't succeed. He thought he knew how to treat a woman; or at least how to treat the hot-house-flower kind of woman who wanted the best of everything—presents, clothes, and jewels—but Catriona found it overpowering.

All that week the chauffeur brought her home, much later than usual, so that Catriona merely put her head round the sitting-room door to say goodnight, then went straight up to her room to get some sleep before getting up early again the next morning. She took care not to be alone with Lucas, working near someone else at the dig and sitting in the back of the car when they drove to and from the site. He was aware of where Omar had taken her, though, because Mike had asked her in front of him and she'd had to answer. Lucas didn't say anything at the time, but on Thursday evening, after they'd finished their meal, he stopped her as Catriona was about to leave the room and waited until the others had gone before he said, 'I've arranged a trip to the temple at Esna for you tomorrow.'

'Tomorrow? Oh, I'm afraid I can't. I've already arranged to go on a felucca trip with the girls.'

'The girls—and Omar?'

Catriona nodded, not meeting his eyes.

'Then I'm sure they can manage without you,' Lucas said smoothly.

'Tomorrow is Friday,' she pointed out rather tartly.

'So?' Lucas folded his arms and leaned against the doorway, giving the impression of being bored.

'So Friday is supposed to be my day off.'

'Which is why I've arranged this trip for you. You can't expect me to help you to improve your knowledge of ancient Egypt on days when you're supposed to be working, now can you? And this is a trip that you'll find very useful in your career,' he said tauntingly. Adding, 'That's if you're still interested in a career, of course.'

He had her over a barrel and he knew it, darn the man. 'Of course I am.'

'Good, then be ready to leave at seven.'

Lucas went to turn away but Catriona said, 'Can't we go to Esna on Saturday instead? I've hardly seen the Nile and I've never been on a felucca; I was really looking forward to the trip—and so were the girls.'

'Are you saying that Omar will cancel the trip if you don't go?'

Catriona thought about it, wondering if Omar would actually go as far as disappointing the girls, then she shrugged. 'I don't know.'

He gave a thin smile. 'Ring him and tell him you can't make it tomorrow,' he instructed. 'Maybe you'll learn something.'

He walked away and for a few moments she stared after him before going into his office to phone Omar. Lucas followed her into the room just as she was putting the receiver down. 'Well?'

'The felucca trip has been put back to next Friday,' she said shortly.

She went to leave but Lucas put out a hand to stop her. 'So now you know whose benefit this and all the other trips this week were for.'

She hesitated, then said, 'I already knew.'

'And I suppose you're enjoying every minute.' Putting out a long finger he touched the gold ankh at her neck and added sardonically, 'And all the gifts.'

She tossed her head away, her rich fair hair swinging. Strangely wanting to goad him, she snapped, 'Of course.'

'I've warned you to be careful, Catriona.'

'I am being careful—of you,' she exclaimed defiantly.

His eyes sharpened. 'Now that's an interesting remark, and maybe explains why you've been freezing me out lately. What makes you think you have to be careful of me—or maybe it's Omar who's warned you off? Just what has he been saying, Catriona?'

'Why, what should he have told me?'

Putting his hands on her shoulders, Lucas said, 'Don't fence with me; if Omar is accusing me of something then I want to know what it is.'

'He hasn't—not directly.'

'I see. Just subtle insinuations, then. But you believed him?' She avoided his eyes and didn't answer. His grip tightened a little. 'Don't you trust me, Catriona?'

She was still for a long moment, then slowly raised vulnerable, green-flecked eyes to look at him. 'I don't know. I don't know you well enough, and—and...'

'Well?' he said impatiently.

She wanted to ask him if he was just using her as a pawn between himself and Omar, but didn't have the courage to ask in case he lied. 'It's nothing, it doesn't matter.'

Lucas gave a short laugh. 'When a woman says that, it always means it's something that really does matter. So what is it, Catriona?'

That revealing remark made her voice harden as she said, 'You know a lot about women, don't you?'

He frowned. 'Is that what's troubling you?' The frown deepened. 'Is it what Omar has insinuated?'

'Is it true?'

His mouth drew into a wry smile. 'I'm thirty-three years old; how many men of that age are inexperienced? And, besides, would you want a man who was completely naïve?'

'No.' Catriona shook her head. 'But I wouldn't want a man who was—who was the opposite.'

'Are you afraid to come right out and say it? I'm not a womaniser, a libertine, or whatever you're thinking. But I am experienced, Catriona, and nothing can change that. I am what I am.' He paused, his eyes holding hers, waiting for her to speak. When she didn't he straightened up and let go of her shoulders. 'I can't make you trust me,' he said harshly. 'That's up to you. You'll have to make up your own mind.' Again he looked at her, but she could only stare up into his face, and after a moment that seemed to go on forever he turned sharply and walked out of the room.

Catriona joined him with some trepidation the next morning, but Lucas greeted her without any apparent animosity. He talked to her on the journey and seemed amicable enough, but she sensed a slight withdrawal in him, and intuitively knew that he was waiting for her to apologise or make some move towards him. Perversely, she didn't, instead maintaining the coolness she had shown towards him all that week.

Esna turned out to be quite a large town on the banks of the Nile, about fifty miles or so south of Luxor. The temple there was in the middle of the town, the buildings round it having grown in height over the last thousand years until the temple was almost covered in soil and sand, only the tops of the columns and the roof being visible until the late nineteenth century, when it was excavated. Now it lay thirty feet below the level of the modern town. All this Lucas told her as they drove along, but he told her in the manner of a teacher instructing a pupil, his tone impartial.

It wasn't until they were inside the temple and he began to describe the inscriptions and translate the ancient hieroglyphs that he made history come alive for her again. The columns had floral capitals, giving the illusions of plants stretching to the sky. And on them was inscribed an account of the rituals of the temple, a calendar of feasts and hymns to the gods. There were so many gods in Egyptian legend and they took so many forms that Catriona had become hopelessly confused, but Lucas made them all seem simple and straightforward, so that she listened eagerly and forgot her coolness as she asked questions, knowing that he would always have the answers.

When they'd seen the temple he took her for a walk through the town, the thronged narrow streets full of open market-like stalls, of piles of garlic onions six feet high, of men in white robes with all types of turbans on their heads. There were women wearing the traditional black robes but with modern plastic flip-flops on their feet; bright-eyed, curly-haired children who came running up to stare at Catriona, to smile at her and touch her hand.

The town was full and so noisy; everyone seemed to be shouting and all the cars and battered trucks honked their horns the whole time. The noise battered at her ears, and the smells of camel and spices and people filled her nostrils. It was all so strange and exciting. This sprawling ant-hill of a town was a new, but very old world, and one, Catriona realised, to which Omar would never have taken her in a million years. They went for lunch to an old rest-house and sat on a balcony under the shade of woven palm leaves. The proprietor, now an old, gnarled man, sat in a chair and held up a photograph of himself when a very young boy taken with the Earl of Carnarvon, the man who had discovered King Tutankhamun's tomb. For a price the proprietor let the tourists take snapshots of him holding his photograph.

'Is it really of him?' Catriona asked Lucas. 'It could be any child.'

'Does it matter? It's a nice story for the tourists.'

'I thought archaeologists were supposed to be sticklers for the exact truth?'

Lucas shrugged. 'Sticklers for the truth don't have any romance in their souls.'

'Don't tell me you're a romantic at heart?' she said disbelievingly.

'Why shouldn't I be?'

'Because—well, you're just not the type.'

He gave a short laugh. 'Perhaps not—but then, you said only yesterday that you don't know me very well.'

Leaning back in her chair, Catriona looked at him over the top of her glass. 'So tell me about yourself,' she invited.

His eyes flicked to her face, met hers. 'What do you want to know?'

There were a great many things about him that Catriona would dearly have loved to know, but how to come right out and ask such personal questions? She took a drink and afterwards ran her fingertip round the rim of the glass, her eyes lowered as she said, 'Have you ever had an affair with Lamia?'

'With Lamia!' His surprise could only be genuine. 'Good grief, no!' Then his eyes narrowed. 'Has Omar insinuated that I have?'

Quickly she shook her head. 'No. It's just—just the way she looks at you sometimes.'

Lucas's mouth curled in sardonic amusement. 'You should see the way she looks at Omar.'

'Really?' Catriona was intrigued to have her suspicions confirmed. 'You mean——?'

'I don't mean anything—and it's none of your business.' He finished his drink and stood up. 'Let's go.'

Reluctantly she followed him, frustratedly thinking that she'd learnt very little. He'd cut her off before she'd had a chance to ask very much at all, which seemed to be about par for the course where Lucas and his private life were concerned.

He took her to the Tombs of the Nobles, an area near the Valley of the Kings, but which wasn't so popular with the mass of tourists who'd just come for the day, and so wasn't crowded, Here doors were opened for him, too, but whereas Omar had opened them with money and been greeted with deferential servility, Lucas was met by his Egyptian colleagues and treated with open respect. He had no need of guides, did not have to press money into waiting hands. Here he was held in esteem and was shown it.

Catriona found herself far more impressed by this than by Omar's show of power. And she liked the way Lucas shook hands with people at the sites, the men who stood for hours to tear tickets or hold a mirror up to the sun to reflect light into a dark tomb, as well as the important men who were in charge of excavations.

'How long have you been coming out here?' she asked him.

'Ever since I was a schoolboy. My parents brought me here for a holiday when I was fifteen and I was immediately hooked. I managed to get myself on an excavation team as a student for the long vacations, and as soon as I got my degree came out here more or less full-time.'

'Don't you ever go back to England?'

'Yes, of course. I'm affiliated to a university as well as a couple of museums. I go back and give lecture tours from time to time.'

'The people here all seem to know you.'

'Yes, I worked in this area for a couple of years. The tomb I found is near here.'

Catriona looked at him eagerly. 'Can we see it?'

'Are you sure you want to see another tomb?'

'Of course I do.'

As they walked to it Lucas told her how it had been found, playing down his own part, but making it exciting, an adventure almost. To reach it they had to go down a steep, narrow staircase cut in the rock which led to a small, not very interesting chamber.

'I thought this was it,' Lucas told her, 'but then we found this other staircase in the little ante-room.' Again they went down and Catriona had to duck as she entered the tomb itself, then gave a gasp of pleasure. The walls of the chamber were beautifully painted with pictures of the dead man and his wife making the usual offerings to the gods, but the uneven roof was covered by a grapevine, heavy with leaves and bunches of black grapes that even now, three thousand years later, still looked good enough to eat. Catriona exclaimed in delight, 'Oh, how wonderful! How amazed you must have felt when you found it. And how thrilled. To find a place that had been lost for all those hundreds of years.'

'Yes, it was quite something,' Lucas agreed, ducking his head to avoid the ceiling. 'One of the best moments of my life.'

She turned to look at him, wondering if Lucas had brought her here so that she could learn more about him, or was it his way of showing her that he was even more powerful where Egyptology was concerned than Omar would ever be? She had been really enjoying the day, but now it occurred to her that Lucas, who had been disparaging about Omar taking her out merely to impress her, could well be doing exactly the same thing.

To test him she said, in admiring tones, 'How clever of you to find it. And so young, too. It must really have made you a big name among Egyptologists. I'm very impressed.'

'So you sound,' Lucas said sardonically. 'I was just lucky, that's all. It's nothing to go overboard about.' He looked at her. 'Or are you being sarcastic?'

Immediately she felt small and rather silly. She shook her head silently.

'What's the matter, Catriona?' Lucas put a finger under her chin and made her look at him.

She went to say 'Nothing', but remembered the reception that answer got, and hastily changed it to, 'I'm fine. Why, what do you think is the matter?'

He raised his eyes heavenwards. 'A typical female answer.' But then his gaze settled on her face, shadowed in the light of the lamps that lit the chamber so far underground. 'I've always wanted to do this,' he said softly, and bent to kiss her.

She let him, but took a firm hold of her emotions and didn't respond. After a few moments he straightened up and looked into her face. Catriona gave a brittle smile. 'Does it add spice to finding the tomb—bringing your women here?'

Lucas's jaw thrust forward. 'What's the matter— missing Omar?'

Frustration and fury filled her. 'Yes, I damn well am,' she yelled at him, and pushed him out of the way as she ran out of the chamber.

Omar went back to Cairo, and Catriona invited Nadia and Dorreya to the dig one day. She had to ask Lucas's permission, which he gave grudgingly, but as soon as he saw that Omar wasn't with them and met the girls he immediately relaxed and walked round the dig with them, translating when their English wasn't good enough for them to understand what Catriona was saying. The girls loved it; they were allowed to help with the work, washed themselves afterwards at the basin in Catriona's room, and even enjoyed the meal!

Lucas was standing next to her as they waved them off when the chauffeur came to take them home. 'They're nice kids,' he remarked.

'I think so,' Catriona agreed warmly. 'I'm growing very fond of them.'

Lucas gave her a swift glance, went to say something, but then changed his mind and went inside.

Catriona almost called his name, but then she, too, had second thoughts. She had been keeping him at a distance, trying to stick to her resolve, but seeing him walk away from her made her feel suddenly terribly lonely. The truth was that she had liked his kisses and her stupid heart craved for more. She would have liked to go for a stroll with him through the moonlit desert, to talk and touch, to feel his arms round her again. If she'd called him back maybe she would have had all that, very possibly even more, but would she have been any the wiser about whether he really cared for her or not? But there was such an ache inside her that to go on being cool towards him was becoming increasingly difficult.

On Thursday, when they were in the finds room after dinner, Lucas casually asked her if she was still going on her felucca trip the next day.

'Why, yes, it's all fixed up. We're leaving around eleven and having a picnic somewhere.'

'Then you might as well ring Omar and tell him not to bother to send his car for you; I have business in Luxor and I can drop you off.'

'OK. Thanks,' she accepted, hiding her surprise at his offer.

She dressed carefully the next day, in a new cream linen dress that she'd made for herself on Mrs Aziz's sewing machine while the girls were resting. It was sleeveless but had a full skirt, so satisfying both Arabic propriety and her own taste. With it she had a straw hat she'd bought in the bazaar and bound with a gaily-coloured silk scarf that Omar had bought for her before she'd learned not to admire things.

Lucas's eyes ran over her when she came out to join him.

'Well?' she demanded.

'Well what?'

'You can't look at me like that and then not say anything.'

His eyes crinkled in amusement. 'You look very——' he deliberately hesitated '—very suitable.'

Suitable for what? she wondered. For a trip on the river, for Omar, or as the girls' tutor? She could take it how she liked, she supposed. She gave him an old-fashioned look, but didn't pursue it. Lucas was quite smartly dressed himself today, in well-cut but casual clothes that Catriona hadn't seen before. And he seemed in a cheerful mood, too.

He drove the Land Rover into the courtyard of the Garden of the Nile and pulled up at the door. Nadia and Dorreya had been watching for the car and came running to meet Catriona. Lucas got out and the girls greeted him, too, gravely shaking hands; they liked him since their day at the site but were still somewhat in awe of him. While Lucas was talking to them Omar also strolled through the door.

'Catriona.' Taking her hand, he bent to kiss it lightly. 'Good morning, Dr Kane. I must thank you for your hospitality towards my daughters.'

'It was a pleasure,' Lucas answered, smiling at the girls. 'They were a great help.'

Catriona expected him to leave then, but he seemed in no hurry, leaning against the Land Rover as he said, 'So you're taking a trip on a felucca?'

'That's right,' Omar admitted.

'What a pleasant way to spend the day; I've always wanted to do that myself.'

Catriona could hardly believe her ears, and glanced quickly at him. But Lucas, with a very bland smile on his face, was looking at Omar expectantly. The latter frowned and said, 'Yes, just a simple *family* outing,' and he emphasised the word 'family'.

But Lucas ignored the heavy hint and gave one of his own. 'I'm so glad Nadia and Dorreya enjoyed themselves at the dig.'

'Catriona said that you had business in Luxor; you mustn't let us keep you,' Omar returned smoothly.

'Unfortunately the man I was to meet has had to cancel the appointment—so I'm at a loose end today.'

'"A loose end"?' Omar pretended not to understand.

'I have nothing to do,' Lucas translated. With outrageous impudence he smiled at the little girls. 'I shall be all alone while you're on your boat trip.'

Nadia understood and pulled at her father's hand, making him lean down while she whispered to him, all the while glancing at Lucas.

Omar straightened. 'As you are *so alone*,' he emphasised, 'my daughters would like to invite you to join us on our boat trip.' There was scarcely veiled anger in his tone and it was obvious that he didn't like the way he'd been manoeuvred into giving the invitation.

'Why, thank you.' Lucas smiled at Nadia. 'I'd like to very much.'

'I will instruct Mrs Aziz to increase the size of the picnic.' And Omar went into the house.

As soon as he'd gone Catriona said to Lucas, 'May I have a word with you?' and walked round the other side of the car out of earshot of the girls. 'Just what the hell are you playing at?' she demanded tersely.

Lucas gave her a look of surprised innocence. 'Playing at?'

'Don't try to bluff me. I bet you never even had an appointment today; in fact, as it's Friday, it's extremely unlikely. You must have planned this all along.'

'Anyone would think you didn't want me to join you,' Lucas complained, not attempting to deny it.

'I don't!'

His eyes hardened. 'Why? Because you'd rather be alone with Omar?'

'Hardly alone,' she retorted.

'So why all the fuss?'

Catriona stared at him, her cheeks flushed. 'Just what are you trying to do?'

'Have a pleasant day out, that's all.'

He moved away from her as he saw Omar come out again, and just for a moment Catriona saw his eyes grow

cold as he looked at the other man. She felt a *frisson*
of fear; Lucas had deliberately arranged this and she
was terribly afraid he meant to have some kind of con-
frontation with Omar. That he should do so in front of
her and the children, the children most of all, filled her
with anger and dread. She shot Lucas a glance of open
fury before she crossed to Omar's side and began to talk
to him, smiling up at him as she did so to let him know
that this was none of her doing.

Lucas's flamboyant display of urbane impudence so
angered Catriona that she was much friendlier and nicer
to Omar than she would normally have been. She had
always respected Lucas's warning and had tried to hold
Omar at a distance, but now she laughed and talked with
him, treating him as a friend and an equal, certainly not
as an employer. He raised his eyebrows a little, but immediately understood and smiled as he took full advantage of the situation.

Lucas, though, satisfied that he had got his way,
seemed not at all put out, and gave most of his attention
to Nadia and Dorreya as they walked down through the
garden, out of a gate at the back and down a short track
to where a felucca awaited them at Omar's private
landing stage. These small boats, with their one white
sail, had always seemed to Catriona like graceful water
birds that glided along the river. Two men in the usual
white robes and turbans helped them aboard and they
sat on seats along the sides of the boat, Catriona sitting
with Dorreya in between her and Omar, Lucas and Nadia
opposite.

If the men felt antagonistic towards each other, they
concealed it, and the female members of the party
enjoyed the sail, exclaiming at buffaloes bathing in the
river, some of them almost submerged so that at first
they looked like crocodiles until a large ear came up to
flip away a fly. They saw cows, and herds of sheep and

goats guarded by a shepherdess wearing a veil sewn with her dowry of gold coins. Bare-footed children ran down to the water's edge whenever they passed a village, dozens of them, all waving and shouting a greeting. They all waved back, but what a contrast between the girls in the boat and those on the bank.

At lunchtime they moored and had their picnic in the patterned circle of shade beneath a palm tree, the sound of water being pumped from the river by means of an Archimedes screw, the same way it had been pumped for thousands of years, tinkling away in the background. Then one of the sailors, sitting a few yards apart from them, took out a lute and began to play, increasing the magic.

The breeze on the river had carried them along at a brisk rate, but when they got in the boat to go back the wind fell and the sailors had to tack to catch it, but then it died altogether and the men had to get out rough wooden oars and row. It was very hot, the sun beating down on their heads. All of them wore a hat of some sort, but Catriona, who was sitting with the girls in the centre of the boat now, so that they were under the shade of the limp sail, began to feel concerned for the two sailors and took a bottle of mineral water from the coolbox and made them stop to take a drink.

'They are used to it,' Omar said dismissively in English. 'Do not worry about them.'

Catriona gave him an indignant look. 'They're middleaged men. How would you like to have to row in this heat?'

'He wouldn't like it at all,' Lucas said with a grin.

'Or you?' she flashed at him.

He grinned again, stood up and took off his shirt. 'Then let's find out.' And he motioned the eldest of the sailors to give up his seat to him.

The man hesitated, looking at Omar, whose face grew tense with anger. But then he gave a disdainful shrug. 'By all means row if it pleases you, Dr Kane.'

'Aren't you going to help?' Catriona asked him.

Omar's head came up, fastidiously proud. 'If you were an Egyptian woman you would not even ask that question. I do not do the work of servants.'

Lucas laughed and told both men to get out of the way, then he took the two oars in his strong hands and began to row.

Catriona sat with the girls in a stunned silence. Soon the sweat of effort broke out on Lucas's skin, began to trickle down his bare chest and straining muscles. His eyes were on her, and didn't waver. Catriona licked lips that had suddenly gone dry. She felt a surge of aching desire and knew a longing to lick the sweat from his heaving chest, to run her hands over his bulging muscles and hot skin. Desire grew into a deep-down, all-consuming flame, but the emotion that filled her was far more than just sensuality. A great surge of exhilaration filled her and Catriona wanted to laugh and cry. Her eyes lit with a new radiance and her heart filled with bursting happiness and pride. I'm in love, she thought. For the first time in my life I'm really in love. But she lowered her eyes so that Lucas wouldn't see.

CHAPTER EIGHT

THE felucca fairly scudded along as Lucas bent to the oars. Catriona turned to look at the bank, her back to the others as she struggled with this sudden enlightenment, this new awareness of her feelings. She gripped the side of the boat, her thoughts in turmoil, her emotions chaotic. One moment she was buoyant with happiness, the next plunged in despair. Just because she was in love with Lucas, it didn't mean that his feelings and actions towards her were any different. She was still as unsure of him as before; in fact, his ploy in coming along today seemed to be merely to goad Omar into anger. And his accepting her challenge to row when Omar had turned it down—was that, too, simply meant to annoy his host?

Reluctantly she turned back to look at the two men. Omar's face was a taut mask of scarcely suppressed rage. His hands gripped the side of the boat as tightly as hers had done, and he, too, had his eyes fixed on the bank. Catriona, trying desperately to hide the surge of emotion she felt, turned her eyes to Lucas. He kept up the same pace but his breath had begun to rasp in his throat and his body glistened with sweat. Catriona stared at him helplessly, wanting to stop this, but knowing that to do so would only infuriate him. She looked to the sailors for help, but they were gazing in awe and astonishment at Lucas as he rowed on beneath the blazing sun. There would be no help from Omar; he'd let Lucas die before he'd do anything. Catriona looked wildly round and then gave a relieved cry. 'Look!' She pointed to the sail. 'The wind's got up again.'

She gestured to the sailors and they immediately ran to the ropes. Lucas stopped rowing and leant on the oars, wiping the sweat from his eyes and getting his breath back. Catriona saw the sailors look at him, respect and admiration in their eyes, and her own silly heart was overwhelmed with pride that she was afraid to show. Lucas didn't speak before shipping the oars and moving to sit on the opposite seat again and put on his shirt. It was then that he looked at Catriona, but she had taken the opportunity to put on her sunglasses and pull her wide-brimmed hat lower so that no one could see anything of her face.

The rest of the journey went by in silence, but Catriona was glad of it because it gave her time to think. She couldn't, she realised, go on as before. If Lucas took her in his arms again, if he kissed her—then she knew she would be lost. There would be no way then that she could hide her feelings; he would know that she'd fallen for him. And she wasn't sure that he wouldn't take advantage of the situation, for his own satisfaction, or to flaunt it in Omar's face. Both perhaps. But that was the trouble, the same problem she'd had to face all along; she just wasn't sure. A great inner sigh racked her. If only there were some way she could find out. Catriona glanced at both men, their enmity apparent now, and it was then an idea came to her. A desperate and risky idea. But she had to know how Lucas really felt about her, and this was the only way she could think of that might work. If she could use their antagonism, use Omar to make Lucas jealous, then Lucas might get angry enough to say what he really felt. But did she dare? Her body tensed as she thought it through. Omar probably wouldn't take kindly to being used, and if she didn't succeed with Lucas... Catriona's face blanched at the thought, realising that she would have to encourage Omar to make Lucas really jealous, to convince him that she wasn't just playing some game. For a moment her heart failed her and she wondered if it wouldn't be better to just sit back and wait, hope to find out. But love was impatient as well as blind. Catriona had never been afraid of a challenge and she decided to risk everything on this one desperate throw. And now, when the enmity between the two men was out in the open, would surely be the best time to start.

They reached the Garden of the Nile and walked round to the front of the house, the little girls subdued as they sensed their father's anger. Omar sent the girls in to Mrs Aziz and stood on the step to say goodbye to Catriona. Lucas opened the door of the Land Rover for her to get in. Taking a deep breath, Catriona pretended to be furious. Taking off her sunglasses, she turned towards him, hazel eyes blazing as she said tersely, 'I'm not going with you.'

Lucas's eyes narrowed. 'What do you mean?'

'You heard me; I'm staying here tonight—and maybe longer if I feel like it.'

Omar straightened in surprise and came over to her. 'Of course, my dear. You must stay as long as you wish.' He threw a triumphant look at Lucas and put a familiar hand on Catriona's arm. She cringed at his touch but didn't shake him off.

'Don't be a fool.' Lucas squared his shoulders and clenched his fists.

Afraid that they might come to blows, Catriona said to Omar, 'Would you leave us for a minute, please? I'd like to talk to—to Dr Kane alone.'

'You will come to the house?' Omar gave her a searching look.

'I've said I will,' she almost snapped back.

'Very well.' Bending his head, Omar kissed her hand lingeringly, an action that was meant to infuriate Lucas.

It did. He took a stride towards him, but Catriona stepped between them and glared up at him, her eyes daring him to do it. Lucas stopped and put his hands on his hips.

'How *dare* you ruin the day for the girls?' she flung at him as soon as Omar had gone inside. 'And don't try to deny it,' she cut in as he went to open his mouth. 'You came along today with the express intention of making a nuisance of yourself. I don't know what's between you and Omar and I don't care, but I——'

'*You're* between us,' Lucas broke in. 'I don't want you to be hurt when you realise what——'

'Rubbish!' Catriona said furiously. 'You were at loggerheads before I even came to Egypt. And how *dare* you bring me into it? You're just using me as an excuse to get back at him. But what makes me even angrier is that you chose to bring things to a head in front of those two children. It was they who wanted you to come along and you abused their hospitality shamefully. So just clear out, Lucas. Go away! I don't care if I never see you again!'

'Women always say that when they don't mean it. Don't be an idiot, Catriona.' He took hold of her arm. 'Listen to me.'

'No! Go away.' She hit out at him in sudden, genuine anger for what he was forcing her to do. So suddenly that she took him by surprise and he was fractionally too slow to stop her. The sound of the slap seemed terribly loud in the quietness of the garden. For a moment they stared at each other, both taken aback by the violence of her feelings, but then, before he could react, Catriona turned and ran into the house, slamming the big door behind her.

Later, she rather bitterly supposed that it was only natural that Omar should take full advantage of the situation. She'd showered and tidied herself in the room she thought of as hers, then went to have dinner with the girls, but Mrs Aziz told her that they were tired after not having their usual lunchtime nap, and she was giving them supper in bed. So, after she'd prolonged saying goodnight to them for as long as possible, Catriona had to go downstairs, feeling more than a little wary.

Omar was waiting for her in the sitting-room. He immediately came up to her, took both her hands in his to kiss them, and kept hold of her hands as he said, 'I am so happy that you're staying here tonight.'

'Look, don't start getting any ideas,' she said quickly. 'I just didn't want to go back with Lucas, that's all.'

'I am not surprised. Dr Kane behaved very badly. Let us have a drink.' He got her one and set out to be charming and attentive to her all that evening and through dinner. He even started to talk of the future, of things they would do together, places they would go.

'The girls will be going back to Cairo to go to school soon, won't they?' she queried.

'Yes, in two weeks.' Omar reached across the table and put his hand over hers, looked into her eyes, his own dark and expressive. 'But that doesn't mean that we have to part. I want you to stay here, Catriona, my beautiful one. To make this your home.'

She put her hand under the table, afraid now. He seemed to think that her rejection of Lucas meant that she preferred him. But that was what she was playing for, wasn't it? 'You mean you want me as a permanent tutor to the girls?' she asked cautiously.

He laughed. 'If you choose to think of it like that. But I think you know what I am saying; I have long admired your beauty and wanted you, Catriona. Surely you know that? Why else have I come here to see you so often?'

'The girls——' she began.

He misunderstood. 'They are very fond of you. It would be wonderful for them to have you here to be with them during all the holidays. And I will find you a flat in Cairo for when they are at school. I will give you everything a woman could want, my fair one. You will have clothes and jewels, a car. We will all go on holidays together. We will teach the children to ski; they would enjoy that, don't you think?'

'Yes.' She looked at him uncertainly, wondering if she'd been wrong about him. 'Omar—are you proposing to me?'

'Proposing?' His voice changed a little, became wary.

'Are you asking me to marry you?' Catriona said bluntly.

He drew back. 'No, Catriona, I cannot ask you to marry me. For a wife I must take an Egyptian, or at least an Arab, woman.'

'But it's OK to take a Western woman as a mistress,' she said acidly.

'I'm not free to choose where I will, my darling. I must marry to please my family and honour my name.'

Forgetting the role she'd set herself, Catriona pushed her chair back angrily. 'I may not be good enough to be your wife, Omar, but I'm sure as hell too good to be your mistress!'

She began to stride towards the door, but he called, 'Catriona! Please, wait.'

She stopped, fuming. 'Well?'

'The children love you. You will be my wife in everything but name. That, alas, I cannot give you now, but perhaps in time, when East and West become closer...' He put his hand on her shoulder. 'People don't get married so much now in the West; would living with me be so much different from such a union in your own country?'

Inwardly thinking that she'd rather die, Catriona nevertheless realised that she needed to string him along for a while, so said shortly, 'Not everyone goes along with that. I have principles, and I have a family, too, you know.'

'Of course,' he said soothingly. 'But please, won't you think about it? For my sake? For Nadia's and Dorreya's?' He went to put his arms round her and kiss her but she turned her head away, knowing she couldn't take that, and he had to be content with her hand. When he straightened there was heat in Omar's eyes. Almost possessively, he said, 'You are beautiful in my eyes, Catriona. I want you for my own.'

She looked at him but didn't speak, just nodded and walked to the door. There she turned and said warningly, 'Don't try to come to my room.'

If he was disappointed, he managed to conceal it. 'Of course not. Not until you say.'

There were dark shadows of sleeplessness around Catriona's eyes the next morning. She had tried very hard to put Lucas out of her mind, but found it impossible. Why she had fallen for him, she couldn't think. He might help with her career of course, which she would probably need more than ever once he had grown tired of her and cast her aside for someone else, she thought in disillusion. Lucas had never said that he loved her, and had even treated her quite roughly on one or two memorable occasions, but when Lucas kissed her it stirred a fire within her and just—just made her want to go to bed with him.

That honest admission cost Catriona another couple of hours' sleep and she wasn't her bright self when she joined Omar and the girls for the drive into Luxor where they were to have lunch. Omar gave her a quick glance but beyond a small smile she managed to avoid his eyes, although from the way he looked at her and touched her whenever he could, she knew that he was waiting eagerly for her answer and expected it to be a positive one.

On the way back Catriona gazed out of the window, fascinated as always by the passing scene. She was still looking idly out of the window when the car slowed down, a truck packed with kneeling camels in its way. Suddenly Catriona jerked forward, shouted, 'Stop the car!' and opened the door.

Omar in turn shouted, '*Oeff*!' to the driver and the car came to a skidding stop.

Catriona was out before it had stopped moving, and ran across to where a donkey, its bones showing through its skin, was cowering against the wall of a house while a man beat at it savagely with a wooden stick. Catriona barged into him with all her strength and grabbed the stick from his startled hand. She turned on the man, flamingly angry, and would have hit *him* with the stick if Omar hadn't come up behind her and grabbed it out of her hand. 'You cruel, inhuman swine!' Catriona yelled at the man. Then to Omar, 'Have him arrested. Have him thrown in prison!'

By now the man had recovered and he began to shout at her. A crowd could gather in Egypt for no reason at all; when an argument developed they emerged from every corner, and everyone had to have their say at the tops of their voices. White with fury, Catriona gestured to the donkey. 'Look at the poor thing. It's hardly alive. It's starving! And look at the marks on it where that beastly man has hit it.'

'You must let me deal with this.' Omar turned an angry face and listened to the donkey's owner who was shouting and waving his arms about, glaring at Catriona and almost spitting the words out at her from his toothless mouth.

Catriona yelled back at him, but suddenly Omar grabbed her and almost dragged her back to the car. 'I will deal with this,' he said angrily. 'Stay in the car where you belong.'

She went to disobey him, but Omar slammed the door and said something to the driver, who clicked on the electric door locks so she couldn't get out. Fuming, she could only watch from the window and was appalled when she saw Omar handing out money to the donkey's owner. When he got back to the car, he sat in the front with the driver, leaving her alone with the girls who had sat in round-eyed amazement throughout the whole incident.

When they reached the house, Catriona got out of the car, stalked into the study and picked up the phone. Lucas answered the call. 'Come and get me—*now*,' she ordered, and replaced the receiver without explanation.

Omar followed her in and shut the door. 'Catriona, you do not understand.'

'Oh, yes, I do. You saw an animal being cruelly treated and not only wouldn't do anything about it, you actually *condoned* it by giving that damn man money!'

Growing angry himself, Omar said, 'Things are different in Egypt. We do not keep animals as pets; they have to work, and if they cannot or will not work then they are of no use.'

'That donkey couldn't work because it was starving.'

Omar sighed. 'You must accept that things are different here. You must let them lead their own lives. You must turn your eyes away from such things.'

'Will you see that the donkey is taken care of?' she challenged.

'I gave the man some money to buy food for it,' he replied, evading a direct answer.

Realising that it was the most she could expect from him, Catriona said shortly, 'I'm not going to apologise for what I did.'

'I am not blaming you. You did not understand. You will know better now.' Omar smiled and took her hand, began to stroke it, but Catriona drew it away.

'I'm going back to the excavation house.' He immediately began to protest, to try to make her change her mind, but Catriona wouldn't listen. 'No. I have to go back. I need time to think. Tell the girls goodbye for me, will you?'

'But you will come as usual on Monday,' he pleaded. 'You promised to teach the girls until they go back to Cairo.'

Reluctantly, she nodded. 'Yes, all right, I'll come on Monday.'

She left then, walking down to and through the gate instead of waiting in the porch as she usually did. Lucas must have driven on horn and accelerator the whole way because she had only been waiting a short time when he braked to a halt in a cloud of dust in front of her.

'What happened?' he demanded as soon as she got in.

'Nothing. Let's go.'

'If Omar's hurt you in any way...'

'He hasn't. Just drive, will you?'

Looking at her set face, Lucas knew he wasn't going to get anything out of her here, so he started the engine and turned the car. When they'd gone a couple of miles, he drew into the side and said, 'Now tell me.'

She gave a short laugh. 'There's nothing much to tell, really. I just had a lesson in the difference in our cultures today, that's all.'

'Did he try to take you to bed?' Lucas demanded.

Turning her head to glare at him, Catriona said, 'For heaven's sake! Don't men ever think about anything but sex? If you must know, I saw a man beating a donkey that could hardly stand. I went to stop it but Omar had the—the nerve to lock me in the car. He even gave the man money!'

Lucas looked at her incredulously, then burst into laughter.

Catriona immediately hit him. Still laughing, he caught her wrist and said, 'Hey! Stop it, you wildcat,' as she continued to take her anger out on him. 'I'm not laughing at *you*. I can just imagine Omar's face when it happened. The dignified Pasha Rafiq having to do a deal with a peasant!' And he gave a renewed roar of laughter.

Catriona gave him an indignant look that slowly changed to a reluctant grin. 'I must admit he was a bit put out,' she owned.

'And even more so when you walked out on him, I imagine,' Lucas said, grinning. 'And just as he thought he was getting somewhere, I bet.' Letting her go, he put his arm along the back of her seat. '*Was* he getting somewhere?'

'What does it matter to you?' she retorted.

Putting up a finger, he traced the dark shadow under her eyes. 'You look as if you haven't had much sleep.'

She brushed his hand away. 'I didn't go to bed with him, if that's what you're insinuating.'

'I wasn't, but I'm very glad.'

'Why?' She raised challenging eyes to meet his, desperately hoping that he would tell her how he felt.

'Don't you know?'

'No. So why don't you tell me?' she said huskily.

He smiled a little, looking deep into her eyes, and she felt her heart give a crazy lurch. But then he turned away. 'Maybe I will one day.' And to her bitter disappointment he started up the car and drove on. After a few moments he said, 'Didn't Omar offer to take your donkey to the sanctuary?'

With a sigh she accepted the diversion. 'No. Is there one?'

'Mm. It's a charity which is making some progress in helping the poor creatures.' He talked about it until they reached the excavation site, but before she got out of the car, Lucas said, 'You're not going back to that house, Catriona.'

'Yes, I am. I promised to teach the girls until they go back to school.'

'Omar hasn't propositioned you, then?' She didn't answer but went to get out of the car, but Lucas caught her arm. 'Has he?' he demanded harshly.

Hope flared again. 'Yes, if you must know.'

'And you're going back there?' he said incredulously.

'And what if I am? What's it to you?'

But again Lucas wouldn't answer her. His face grew grim and he got out of the car and slammed into the house.

She didn't see much of Lucas during the following week, and, thankfully, she didn't see anything of Omar either, as he had to go back to Cairo. But Omar called her on the phone at his house and sent presents, too: flowers, perfume, some gorgeous lace handkerchiefs. Catriona put the flowers in water, but left the other presents in their boxes, upstairs in her room at the Garden of the Nile. All her spare time was spent in making up one of the dresses she'd designed. It was an evening dress in two parts; a black full-length skirt of minute vertical pleats attached to a gold embroidered waistband, and the top just a very deep collar which came down from her neck to cover her breasts and was linked to the waistband by an embroidered blue and gold lotus flower.

The girls and Mrs Aziz became quite involved with the project and exclaimed admiringly when it was finished. 'You will be able to wear it to the party,' Nadia said excitedly.

'What party?'

'My father always gives a party at the end of the summer. It is to be next week.'

Mrs Aziz shushed her, but Catriona confidently waited for Omar to tell her about it when he came home. He brought her more presents, was eager for her company, acting like any man who wanted a woman—but he didn't mention the party. It was Lamia who brought it up, when they were all sitting having supper at the excavation house one evening. Turning to her husband, she said, 'I must have a new dress to wear to Omar Rafiq's party.' And she gave Catriona a sidelong look. 'He has a big party every year, you know.'

'Yes, I know,' Catriona returned evenly.

'You are going?' Lamia demanded.

How to answer? Catriona's face tightened a little, but before she could speak, Lucas said, 'Of course she's going—with me.'

Lamia pouted but said nothing more, but after the meal Catriona got Lucas alone and said, 'Have you really had an invite to Omar's party?'

'Yes. I get one every year.'

'But surely he wouldn't want you there?'

'He invites everyone of any importance,' Lucas said drily. 'And as I'm the leader of this excavation he has to invite me—and I have to go.'

'Did the invitation include—a friend?'

'You mean did it include you? No, of course not.' Sitting on the edge of his desk, he said, 'He won't invite you, Catriona.'

'Why not?'

'Oh, no.' He gave her a stony look. 'If you can't see it, then you must ask Omar.'

He wouldn't say any more, and the girls and Mrs Aziz had obviously been forbidden to mention it. Catriona could have asked Omar when he called on the phone, but she didn't; she was angry and thought this might have ruined her plan to make Lucas jealous. She didn't want him to feel sorry for her, for God's sake! So she could only hope that if she went to the party with Lucas something might happen between the two men so that she could at last find out the truth.

There was no full-length mirror at the excavation house so Catriona had to make do with standing on a chair to look in the one on the wall. But she thought she looked OK. Her hair she'd taken up into a sophisticated style and had outlined her eyes with black pencil and gold for the lids, the way the women in the ancient wall-paintings always looked. She carried the evening bag that Omar had given her and wore a pair of gold shoes she'd bought in Luxor. And the dress was all she'd hoped.

It certainly made Lucas do a double-take when she walked down the stairs to join him. Lamia and Mohamed had already left and he was waiting alone. His eyes widened when he saw her and for a long moment he didn't speak, just drank her in, but then his features hardened as he said, 'Is all this for Omar's benefit?'

Her head came up. 'No, for mine.'

He grinned at that. 'Well, you're certainly going to have a stunning effect.'

Catriona didn't say so, but she thought Lucas looked quite stunning, too. She'd never seen him in formal evening clothes before; somehow the clothes changed him, made him seem like a stranger, and even more withdrawn. But they certainly suited him, emphasising his height and the width of his shoulders, his tan against the snowy whiteness of his shirt.

She had expected to travel in the old Land Rover, but to her surprise there was a new saloon car waiting outside. His thoughtfulness went to her heart but she managed to hide it. 'Where did you find the pumpkin?' she asked flippantly.

He grinned, getting the allusion at once. 'I have a direct line to the Fairy Godmother.'

'In that case make it a magic carpet next time, please.'

'Will do.'

So the evening started on a light note, but Catriona's heart was beating fast by the time they arrived at the Garden of the Nile. Lights blazed from every downstairs window of the house and coloured lights were strung from the trees in the garden. Fountains, a great extravagance in this land where water was the most precious commodity, sent jets of diamond-bright star-drops into the velvet of the night. There was another fountain in the big open courtyard where the party was being held, although its sound was drowned beneath the beat of a background group of musicians and the gaggle-of-geese-like noise of scores of people each talking loud enough to make themselves heard.

There were several people in front of Lucas and Catriona, waiting to be greeted, but it was a woman who was receiving, a middle-aged woman in an elegant grey dress.

'This is Mrs Rafiq, Omar's mother,' Lucas told Catriona as they shook hands. 'Miss Catriona Fenton.'

Mrs Rafiq nodded courteously, but looked more at her dress than at Catriona, making it quite obvious that she had never heard of her granddaughters' tutor.

They moved on into the courtyard, were given drinks and moved to join the leader of the French dig and his wife. Both tall, both good to look at, especially together, they attracted many eyes as they went. The French archaeologist's wife, herself always chic, went into raptures over Catriona's dress and begged her to make one for her to send to her daughter in France. Catriona was pleased, but wouldn't commit herself. Food began to be served in another room, the crowd cleared a little. Catriona turned her head—and there was Omar, staring at her with a punch-drunk look on his face. Her chin came up—and she turned her back on him.

Lucas had seen; he gave her a frowning glance, but then lifted his eyes to watch Omar as he walked towards them.

'Dr Kane. How kind of you to come.'

'Thank you for asking me,' Lucas returned politely. Adding with irony, 'I expect you remember Miss Fenton.'

'But of course.' Omar bowed over her hand but he didn't kiss it. 'You look very beautiful tonight, Catriona.'

'Thank you,' she answered coldly. 'What a brilliant party; I see that everyone of any importance to you has been invited.'

A distressed look came into Omar's eyes. Leaning forward, he said softly into her ear, 'Please, I must talk with you.'

'Go ahead.'

'Alone,' he said urgently. 'Come to my study in ten minutes. Please, Catriona.' She gave him a sparking glance, realising that he didn't want to openly admit that he knew her. 'I wish to explain,' he went on. 'Please let me do that.'

She had been about to say no, but remembered she was supposed to be making Lucas jealous, so said instead, 'I'll think about it.'

Omar looked as if he would like to persuade her further, but someone came up and spoke to him and he had to turn away.

'What did he want?' Lucas demanded.

'To explain.'

'And are you going to listen to him?'

'I don't know.'

'Which means you will,' Lucas said grimly.

Catriona swung round on him. 'I wish you'd stop making remarks like that. You may think you know about women, but you certainly don't know anything about me!' And she strode away from him, across the courtyard and up the stairs to the gallery where she knew Nadia and Dorreya would be watching, peeping through the banisters. They greeted her with delight, exclaimed in wonder at the dress and were so pleased to see her that it was much more than ten minutes before she left them and went down to Omar's study. She walked slowly, hoping that Lucas would see, would come and stop her, but she didn't see him. Omar was still there, striding impatiently up and down the room.

'At last!' He came forward to take her hands but she put them behind her back. 'You are angry with me.'

She gave a sardonic laugh. 'Angry? When you ask me to share your life and then don't even invite me to your annual shindig! Why on earth should I be angry?'

'You do not understand, Catriona, my darling. I did not invite you because I wished to guard your reputation.'

'What?' She looked at him incredulously.

'People would not have understood our relationship.'

'We haven't got a relationship,' she retorted.

'*That* is what they would not have understood. If you were here, at my side, everyone would think you my mistress.'

'But that's what you want, isn't it?'

'Very much.' His eyes went over her and he put his hand on her bare midriff, but she moved away.

Playing for time, hoping against hope that Lucas would come, she said, 'Am I to take it, then, that if I did stay here with you I'd never be invited to any of your parties?'

'On the contrary; we would give as many as you wished.'

'But your mother and the rest of your family wouldn't come to them; you'd keep us in separate parts of your life?' she guessed shrewdly.

Catching hold of her, Omar said urgently, 'You will soon get used to things, and I will make it up to you, my fair one, my heart's desire.' She went to pull away but he wouldn't let her. 'Catriona, I have kept my word, I have given you time. I have not pushed you for an answer.'

Looking into his eyes, seeing the desire that burnt there, she said, 'But you are now.'

'Yes. Oh, yes. Seeing you tonight, so beautiful, with every man's eyes on you... I want you, Catriona. Say that you will stay here tonight. Promise that you will never leave.'

There was a sharp rap on the door and he hastily let her go.

'Saved by the bell,' Catriona remarked with a laugh of intense relief.

Omar gave a puzzled frown. 'I heard no bell.'

'It was a hypothetical bell.' She looked round, trying to hide the love in her eyes as Lucas came into the room, shutting the door behind him.

'Need any help?' he asked.

'To do what?'

'To tell him to go to hell.' Walking forward, Lucas came to stand in front of Omar, his hands on his hips, glaring at the other man. 'To tell him that I'm not going to let him ruin your life as he tried to ruin Elaine's.'

Catriona gave a small gasp and stood aside, realising that this wasn't about her any more—if it had ever been. With a sick feeling of despair in her heart she knew that Lucas had come to avenge the woman he and Omar had been rivals for before.

'You are making a fool of yourself, Dr Kane,' Omar said shortly. 'Every woman has a choice. Can I help it if Elaine chose me instead of your colleague?'

'Colleague?' Catriona's head came up in startled surprise, but both men ignored her.

'You knew Harry Carson was in love with Elaine so it amused you to take her yourself. You ruined her life and Harry's too.' Lucas took hold of Omar's lapels and jerked him towards him. 'Just as it amused you to flirt with Lamia until you found she was too easy prey. And when you realised that I was falling for Catriona you decided to seduce her, too. But you're not going to get away with it this time, Omar; I'll smash your pretty face in before I let you even touch her. Do you hear me?'

Angrily Omar shook him off. 'All right, Dr Kane, maybe I was amusing myself with Elaine, but I didn't have to seduce her; she was willing enough. More than willing. And as for Catriona——' Omar turned his head to look at her '—what may have started out as an idle amusement has grown into much, much more. I have fallen in love with her. I have offered her my heart and——'

'But not your name,' Lucas cut in. 'So just keep your filthy hands away from my girl!'

'*Your* girl?' Omar looked quickly at Catriona, then laughed as he saw the startled amazement in her eyes. 'But no, I think not, Dr Kane. No woman would choose a man of your rough manners when she could have me. No woman would choose the primitive hut you live in when she could have all this,' and he gave an expansive gesture with his hand.

'No?' Lucas jeered. 'How little you know her. Catriona has too much pride to be taken in by a house packed with luxuries, by a man who doesn't care enough about her to even invite her to meet his mother.'

'I do care,' Omar said in sudden heat. 'Tonight—when I saw her... My darling, you are so lovely.' He reached to take Catriona's hand but Lucas struck it away.

'Don't touch her!'

Omar turned on him in a rage. 'Do not give me orders in my own house! It is for Catriona to say which of us she wants.'

There was a short shattering silence as the two men gazed at each other in furious hatred. It was Lucas who broke it. 'Then *let* her choose,' he said harshly.

They both turned to look at Catriona as she stood staring at them, stunned and wide-eyed. She tried to speak, couldn't, and began to tremble. She'd learnt what she wanted, but in such a way... Why the hell hadn't Lucas come right out and told *her* how he felt? Clenching her hands, Catriona closed her eyes tightly for a moment, then spoke, her voice shaking. But to their amazement it was anger that choked her voice as Catriona said, 'I already have chosen. *I don't want either of you*! What the hell do you think I am; a pawn to be pushed around the chessboard while you two play at being knights? Some sort of prize in a power struggle?' She strode towards the door while they were still too shocked to move. 'I'm going back to England. I'm going to develop my designs and I'm going to become rich and famous. And I sure as hell don't need *either one of you*.' And she slammed out of the door. Then paused to lock it. They could fight each other to a standstill for all she cared!

The airport at Luxor was as empty as it had been on the day that Catriona had arrived. But the night flight was due in soon and she had booked a ticket on it to take her to Cairo. Luckily there had been a taxi outside Omar's house which she had grabbed to take her to the excavation house and made wait while she threw a few

things into a holdall and changed. There was no time
for more; the rest of her things could be sent on to her.
On the way to the airport they passed a couple of cars
tearing along in the other direction, but it was too dark
to see who was in them.

At the airport she went into the Ladies, to brush out
her hair and wash off the exotic make-up, replacing it
with just lipstick. When she came out she saw Omar's
chauffeur looking round for her. As soon as he saw her
he came over and handed her a small black leather case.
'Pasha Rafiq,' he told her. 'He wait outside in car for
you.' She nodded. 'You come?'

'Perhaps.'

She waved him away and when he'd gone opened the
case. Inside was the most breathtaking diamond
necklace! Catriona gulped and stared, then turned
quickly as one of the airport officials came up to her.

'Miss Fenton?'

'Yes.'

'I have a message for you.'

He held out an envelope which bore her name in
Lucas's unmistakable hand. The message inside was short
and was unsigned. 'My love for you is in my heart as
the reed is held in the arms of the wind.'

Catriona looked at it, gave a long sigh and walked
through the airport into the night. There were two cars
waiting. Omar's gleaming Mercedes and the battered
Land Rover. Omar was inside his car but Lucas was
leaning against his as he always did, but straightened,
his body tense, as she walked across to the limo. Omar
got out, eager elation on his face, but it swiftly changed
as she handed him the necklace and said, 'Thanks, Omar,
but the answer is no. I'm afraid it's always been no. Give
my love to the girls and tell them goodbye for me, will
you, please?'

She turned without waiting for him to answer and walked across to the other car. Lucas's eyes were on her face and she saw in them the triumphant love that filled her own heart. But true to character he merely got in the car and waited for her to join him before he said, 'You took your time.'

'So did you.' She leaned back in the seat with a sigh of content as he drove away. 'Where did the quotation come from?'

'It was an extract taken from a letter a man sent to the woman he loved over three thousand years ago.'

Catriona nodded, well pleased, but said teasingly, 'Don't you ever say anything that's original?'

Reaching out, he put his hand over hers. 'I will tonight.'

It was a promise, an avowal, a declaration of love.

'Why didn't you tell me before?' she asked huskily.

'I had to let you make you own choice—but when I thought of you with Omar, of him touching you——' He broke off, his face grim.

Catriona turned her hand in his and he clasped it tightly, letting her know how much he cared, how much it had mattered.

Lucas had to take his hand away as they went round a bend and she lifted her own to wipe away a silly tear.

'What did Omar offer you?' he asked after a moment.

Unable to keep a note of smugness out of her voice, Catriona said, 'A diamond necklace.'

Lucas whistled in surprise. 'And you gave it back.'

'It wasn't to my taste,' she answered simply, but implying a great deal more.

He turned to grin at her, making her heart swell, but then, outrageously, he said, 'You should have kept it; it would probably have kept the dig going for a couple of years.'

She thumped his shoulder in pretended rage, and then they were both laughing, but Catriona said, 'You'll return the sponsorship money to Omar now, won't you?'

But Lucas shook his head. 'I can't. I sent it to Elaine. Omar ruined her life and I don't see why he shouldn't pay for it.'

'So *that's* why you took it! I was afraid...'

'What? That I'd do anything to make Omar angry?'

'That—and to keep the dig going,' she acknowledged.

Lucas shook his head. 'I could fund the dig out of my own money, if I wanted to; my family are quite well-to-do. But I've always preferred to fight for funds in the commercial jungle, just like any other excavation leader. I want to be judged on my own merits, not be accused of having unfair advantages.'

Catriona listened in astonishment. It explained so many things, especially why Lucas had been so contemptuous when he'd accused her of being susceptible to Omar's wealth and position.

'I'm afraid that now you're going to have to take on another job besides your own,' Lucas said, cutting into her thoughts.

'What job?'

'Lamia's. You see, she only runs the house because none of us has a wife to do it, but as we'll be getting married soon you can take over and she can go and live in Luxor.'

'What did you say?' Catriona said faintly.

'But first I thought we'd close the dig down for a month or so while we take a honeymoon,' Lucas continued. 'We have to meet each other's families, and——'

'Hey!' Catriona broke in, tears and laughter mingled now. 'Am I hearing right?'

'What you're hearing is me making a not very good job of asking you to marry me,' Lucas grinned.

'You'd really close down the dig for me?' she asked in awe.

'Of course. It's no longer the first love of my life, you see.'

'Oh, Lucas.'

They reached the excavation house and she expected him to stop, but he drove past and on to the dig. It was the most beautiful night; the moon silvered the sand and cast long shadows where the stone pillars still stood as a tribute to the past.

Lucas took her hand and they walked across to one of the taller columns. 'There used to be an altar here once. Just a small altar in a private temple. I'd like us to be married here.' His eyes crinkled into a tender grin. 'That's if you ever get round to saying yes, of course.'

'Yes, and yes, and yes.'

Immediately he swept her into his arms, kissing her with all the passion of a man who had found long-yearned-for love at last, and found it returned a hundredfold. It was a long time before Lucas loosed his hold enough to say, his voice thick, triumphant, full of happiness, 'I knew Omar had blown it when he wouldn't rescue that donkey.'

Catriona chuckled. 'Oh, no; he wasn't even in the running from the moment you burst into his house and demanded to know what he'd done with your textile expert.'

Lucas gave a crack of laughter. Putting his hands on her waist, he lifted her up and spun her round in jubilant happiness. But then his eyes darkened and he bore her down on to the desert sand to claim his love at last.

RUGGED. SEXY. HEROIC.

OUTLAWS and HEROES

Stony Carlton—A lone wolf determined never to be tied down.

Gabriel Taylor—Accused and found guilty by small-town gossip.

Clay Barker—At Revenge Unlimited, he *is* the law.

JOAN JOHNSTON, DALLAS SCHULZE and MALLORY RUSH, three of romance fiction's biggest names, have created three unforgettable men—modern heroes who have the courage to fight for what is right....

OUTLAWS AND HEROES—available in September wherever Harlequin books are sold.

HARLEQUIN ®

Harlequin Romance ®

AVAILABLE IN OCTOBER—A BRAND-NEW COVER DESIGN FOR HARLEQUIN ROMANCE

Harlequin Romance has a fresh
new eye-catching cover.

We're bringing you an exciting new
cover design, but Harlequin Romance
is still committed to bringing you
warm and contemporary love stories
that are sure to touch your heart!

See how we've changed and look
for these fabulous stories with a
brand-new look:

#3379 Brides for Brothers
by Debbie Macomber
#3380 The Best Man
by Shannon Waverly
#3381 Once Burned
by Margaret Way
#3382 Legally Binding
by Jessica Hart

Available in October,
wherever Harlequin books are sold.

Harlequin Romance ®—
Dare To Dream

HARLEQUIN ⬥ PRESENTS®

Ever felt the excitement of a dangerous desire...?

The thrill of a feverish flirtation...?

Passion is guaranteed with the third in our new selection of sensual stories.

Indulge in...

Dangerous Liaisons
Falling in love is a risky affair!

Next month, watch for:
Shades of Sin
by SARA WOOD
Harlequin Presents #1765

The rebel is back! Four years ago, Natasha had fallen for the local "bad boy," Ruan Gardini. He'd made Natasha come alive for the first time...but it was a turbulent relationship and they'd parted bitter enemies. Now Ruan was back to claim his revenge for the sins of the past, and he was every bit as daring, sexy and irresistible as Natasha remembered!

Available in September wherever Harlequin books are sold.

DL-4

HARLEQUIN PRESENTS®

Dark secrets...

forbidden desires...

scandalous discoveries...

an enthralling six-part saga from a bright new talent!

HEARTS OF FIRE
by Miranda Lee

This exciting new family saga is set in the glamorous world
of opal dealing in Australia. *HEARTS OF FIRE* unfolds over
six books, revealing the passion, scandal, sin and hope
that exist between two fabulously rich families. Each novel
features its own gripping romance—and you'll also be
hooked by the continuing story of Gemma Smith's search
for the truth about her real mother, and the priceless
Black Opal....

Coming next month

BOOK 3: *Passion & the Past*

After the tragic end to her marriage, Melanie was sure she
could never feel for any man again—until Royce Grantham
set his blue eyes on her! Melanie was determined not
to repeat past mistakes...but Royce made her feel
overwhelmed by desire. Meanwhile, Nathan's trusting young
bride, Gemma, had already been seduced by passion—and
was discovering the difference between lust and love....

Harlequin Presents: you'll want to know what happens next!

Available in September wherever Harlequin books are sold.

FIRE4